# A Little Hurt Ain't Never Hurt Nobody

# A Little Hurt Ain't Never Hurt Nobody

## Kimberly T. Matthews

**Urban soul**

## URBAN BOOKS

http://www.urbanbooks.net

This is a work of fiction. Any references or similarities to actual events, real people, living or dead, or to real locales are intended to give the novel a sense of reality. Any similarity in other names, characters, places, and incidents is entirely coincidental.

URBAN SOUL is published by

Urban Books
1199 Straight Path
West Babylon, NY 11704

ISBN-13: 978-1-59983-070-4
ISBN-10: 1-59983-070-1

First Printing: December 2008

10 9 8 7 6 5 4 3 2 1

Printed in the United States of America

*Dedicated to every person
who struggles with embracing the present
because of hurts of the past.*

*Nothing just happens and everything happens for a reason—at least that's what they say. But to save my life, I can't seem to figure out what in the world is going on with me. I would ask God, but right now I'm not speaking to Him, and this is why.*

# Prologue

"Jream, let's do something we haven't done in a long time," my husband, Cade, asked as he eased back on his pillows. Right away I stopped trying to solve the Sudoku puzzle I'd been working on and gave him a sly smile, thinking that he wanted to have sex. It had been a while, for his condition had made him barely able to perform.

"Okay," I said excitedly, putting my puzzle book and pen on the nightstand before snuggling up to him and instinctively letting my hands travel to the places that used to turn him on the most.

"No, babe, not that," he said, gently stilling my hands. A pained expression crossed his face as his eyes studied mine, one at a time.

"What is it, babe?" I asked, pushing away slightly as I circled my thumb on the back of his hand.

In a matter of seconds, the look of pain was replaced by the love and passion I'd seen in his eyes when we'd first met. He didn't have to say it, but the words fell from his lips just the same. "I love you,

Jream," he whispered, tugging at my arm to coax me closer to him.

"I love you too, Cade. You're the love of my life." I pressed a kiss between the scratchiness of his beard just below his jawline. With a soft hand, he stroked my hair, then circled a finger around my ear. With his other hand, he grasped at my fingers, which were tracing a random pattern on his chest.

"Pray with me, Jream," he requested between coughs as he tightened his grip on my hand.

"Of course, babe." I kissed him once more, then closed my eyes, waiting for him to lead the way to the throne room of the Most High. Usually when Cade went to the Lord in prayer, his words were full of power and strength; they would always seep into the crevices of my soul and reassure me that God would see us through any situation—no matter how tumultuous. But this time, Cade sounded like a four-year-old child. I fought to keep from peeling my eyes open when he began to speak.

"'Now I lay me down to sleep, I pray the Lord my soul to keep. . . .'" His voice weakened and became shaky as his words were accented with slight sniffling. "'If I should die before I wake . . .'" There he took a long pause that allowed me time to silently send up my own prayer for his complete healing. "'I pray the Lord my soul to take.'" He squeezed my fingers once more before uttering, "'Amen.'"

"Amen," I agreed, then pressed his fingers to my lips. I smiled to myself, grateful of Cade's love and God's mercy. Cade had been battling lung disease for several months now, but somehow, day by day, he was making it. His all-night coughing hardly kept me awake anymore, and I'd become accustomed to his wheezing. I made sure to keep water by his bedside, along with his prescription medicines. I noticed that he'd been depending on them less and less, and he was optimistic about his recovery, even when sometimes he seemed to be giving up the fight.

Within two minutes, I could feel the weight of his arm increase as he relaxed into a peaceful sleep. "Thank you, Lord," I whispered.

My eyes popped open abruptly at five-fifteen. There was an unusual and eerie chill in the room, although Cade kept our bedroom nice and toasty just for me, even if it meant he was uncomfortably warm. The kids wouldn't be up for another two hours, and although it had always been completely silent in the house this time of morning, even the silence was more silent than normal. Cade was turned over on his right side, his back to me and his right hand gently lay across his left shoulder, which is how he normally slept if he wasn't holding me in his arms.

"Cade," I called softly. "Cade, I'm cold," I added, nestling more beneath the covers. Cade had spoiled me so terribly that me getting up and adjusting the temperature myself was unheard of. "Baby?" It was then that I reached over to nudge him slightly. I felt death's icy sensation shoot through my fingers and travel all over my body in a split second, although I'd immediately drawn my hand back with a horrified gasp. "Cade! Cade, wake up!" I called out to my husband, but I knew he was gone. My tears were instant as I leapt to my feet, scurried to his side of the bed and fell to my knees, bringing my face close to his.

Fighting against the lifeless coolness of his skin and the rigor mortis that had already settled in, I draped one arm around his shoulder and rested my forehead against his cheek, letting my tears wash over his flesh. For the next hour or so, I stayed in that position, thinking about everything, and nothing, all at the same time. My husband was gone. But how could this be? Hadn't God heard my prayers, and wasn't he getting better?

Right before I stood to my feet to leave Cade's side, anger began to set in. I'd asked Cade several times in simple conversations not to leave me. He'd always smile, even when he barely had the strength to do it, and say, "Why would I ever do a fool thing like that, Jream?" I'd smile back, peck his lips, we'd whisper "I love you," promising that we'd always be by each other's side. And as long as death and life were in the power of the tongue—despite his health—I didn't expect Cade to die anytime soon. But he'd done it anyway. He just slipped away in the middle of the night without so much as a kiss good-bye.

I'd also earnestly asked God not to take him. "Not yet, Lord," I'd prayed after the doctor had stated a dreadful "no more than six months." I'd asked, "Please just give us a little more time. Don't force our babies to grow up without a daddy. God, if you be God, let Cade live."

But what did God do? He ignored me. Just took

him regardless of my tears and fervent prayers that were supposed to avail much.

And for that, I was mad at Him too. Cade was gone, so I couldn't *not* be speaking to him, but God? I just didn't want to hear anything He had to say.

# Chapter 1

"Caryn, don't forget that CJ gets out of school early today, so make sure you come straight home," I yelled up the stairs as I rushed to the kitchen in search of my keys so I could get to work.

"Okay," my sixteen-year-old daughter yelled back. Caryn was the spitting image of her daddy, other than the fact that she was a female. Her dark eyes, defined cheekbones, full, round lips and thick (only manageable by a good relaxer) tresses—to name only a few of Cade's definable features—sometimes haunted me to the point that I had to turn my head away from Caryn and fight back tears. Either that, or hold her in my arms until she pleaded for release.

"And I'm taking out some ground beef so you can make some cheeseburgers this evening for dinner. I shouldn't be too late tonight," I added, coming back into the kitchen and heading for the refrigerator. There was a pause, with no response. "Did you hear me?"

"Yes, Mom."

"Well, next time acknowledge me," I replied,

keeping my cool. "And you make sure you behave yourself in school today." I kissed CJ on his forehead as he gobbled a toaster pastry and an orange, which I'd cut into quarters.

"I will, Mom," he promised, hugging my neck tightly. "And you have a good day at work, and don't let your employees get on your nerves."

I had to laugh out loud as I tussled through his curly hair. "What do you know about employees?" I was going to start watching my conversations around this kindergartener. "I'll see you when I get home, babe. Love you."

"Love you too, Mom. Can I watch *Power Rangers* until it's time for my bus?"

"No, watch *Sesame Street* and *Clifford,*" I said just before opening and closing the door that led to the garage.

In a matter of seconds, I was seated in my vehicle and backing out onto the driveway and then the street. At the push of a button, my car was filled with the laughter coming from the local radio's morning show DJs. The comical staff was on the phone with a woman who shared that when she'd lost her husband, she'd swiftly moved on to dating another man within a month of saying her final farewells at her husband's funeral.

"He was gone, I can't raise the dead, can I?" she asked with no apprehension.

"Let me just ass-you diss," the host began with a guffaw. "What you do wit' that man's insurance money?"

"'That *man's* insurance money'?" she repeated, emphasizing "man's." "That money wasn't his! That money was for me! Let me tell you something, don't nobody leave this world with they-own insurance money!"

"I know that's right!" quipped one of the DJs in the background.

"If it was his, then the check woulda been made out to him, right?"

"I guess you got a point there," another DJ responded.

"But it wasn't. It was made out to me! And I took that money and bought me a new car, paid off all our bills and had enough left over to go on a cruise and go shopping when I got back."

"Did you take your new man witchu on the cruise?" the DJ poked.

"I sure did!" the woman admitted unashamedly, which caused an eruption of more laughter from the show staff, while the DJ hollered out: "Oh, Lawd! Did you even cry? Did you shed one tear over the man?"

"Yeah, I cried, but—" I turned the radio off, not caring to hear the rest of the woman's response, and thought about how I'd dealt with Cade's death.

With Cade gone, I certainly hadn't jumped back into the dating scene, but I avoided being at home as much as I could and spent almost every waking minute at my lingerie shop, Sweet Jream's. Staying at home had just been too painful, and it wasn't like the shop didn't need the extra attention.

Sweet Jream's had really been struggling for the last few years to stay out of the red, seemingly regardless of the efforts I'd put toward its potential

success. One of the main reasons for its lackluster
performance was the store had not really been inviting. In retrospect, I realized that with garments jum-
bled about on thin plastic hangers, or lying out on
a table, it didn't look much different than an unor-
ganized beauty supply store. I didn't take a cruise or
buy a new vehicle, but the very first thing I did was
to have the store completely renovated and remod-
eled with the money Cade left behind in the form of
insurance policies. I purchased the space next
door and had the walls separating the two spaces
knocked down. What had been one thousand square
feet of plain beige walls—holding scantily clad
plastic body forms dressed in bras and panties and
other garments, positioned here and there—simple,
partially rusted merchandise racks and worn-out,
dirty beige commercial carpet, featuring several
spills, had been transformed into three thousand
square feet of rich, luxurious shopping space. It instantly gave any woman a feeling of pampering
when she set foot in the store.

I'd called in professional interior designers to
decorate the store in a beautiful Moroccan theme of
red, purple and gold. Beaded chandeliers hung from
the ceiling, which had been painted a midnight blue
and embellished with small sparkly rhinestones,
creating an incredible ambiance, whether day or
night. The bland, flat tables that either held display
merchandise or hid boxes of back stock items had
been replaced by hand-painted, buffet-style cabi-
nets. And now, full-size manikins stood about the
store showing off their figures of various sizes and
curves. Intimate settings of plush, comfortable arm-

chairs and sofas were cozily positioned in a few nooks. Thick carpeting covered the floors, with patterned rugs protecting the heavy-traffic areas, and customers were encouraged upon entrance to slip out of their shoes and into a pair of soft, disposable Pedi-Foam slippers.

My favorite upgrade was a king-sized bed featuring a handmade, hand-painted Moroccan headboard enhanced with a mountain of pillows underneath a glittery gold netting, which discouraged customers from lying on it—in most cases—but really was the accent that brought the entire theme together and helped the store really look like its name. Sweet Jream's now really did look like a dream . . . my dream.

After several long days and nights of renovations, planning, marketing, creating flyers, sending out mailers, collecting e-mail addresses and sending out teasers, sending out e-newsletters and spying on my competitors, a grand reopening was scheduled. I'd promoted Michetta and Shanice to manager and assistant manager, respectively, hired on a couple more sales associates—Grace, Tweet and Taylor—and implemented a dress code of all black, accented with gold, to give us a more polished and sophisticated image.

And in the snap of a finger, the success of Sweet Jream's had skyrocketed. The Saturday morning of our grand opening, I had never seen so many women crowd into my store in my life. From the time we turned back the lock at nine in the morning, there was an influx of women, some with their significant others, all oohing and aahing at the new décor and ready to spend their hard-earned dollars.

Most of our return customers didn't even notice or seem to mind the slight price increase, and we were kept very busy ringing up purchases, swiping credit cards and thanking shoppers for their business.

That evening, after the doors had closed, I tallied the money while the girls replenished the sales floor from the back stock inventory. In between, we had a mini celebration, clinking together plastic champagne glasses of Sprite and gobbling down delectable truffles and dark-chocolate- and white-chocolate-covered strawberries, which I had had catered for the customers.

"Jream, you've really turned this place around!" Michetta said through a mouthful of white chocolate as she restocked a collection of thongs.

"Yes, you did," Shanice then shouted over the whirr of the vacuum cleaner. "The store is hot!"

"Thanks, ladies. I couldn't have done it without your help, though."

We got the store prepped for the next day's opening, gathered our things, including the bank bag filled with cash for a night deposit, and left. "Thanks again! I appreciate you so much," I said, hugging both ladies before I finally sank into the seat of my car. As a general rule, and for our safety, we'd wait until each person got safely in her vehicle and started her engine, and then we'd all pull out together. That night, however, I waved them on, just needing a few minutes to rest and think through the day, which had really exceeded my expectations. I let out an exhausted, yet exhilarating sigh, leaned back against the head rest and smiled. It was the first time I had smiled in ages.

\* \* \*

The store's performance had been continually stellar since its opening three months ago, and it gave me a reason to live again. The months it took to complete the renovations and reopen the store was the distraction I felt I needed to pack away my feelings regarding Cade's passing, but reality always sank back in at the end of the day—no matter how much I busied myself with the duties of its maintenance and operation. The day always ended with me having to go home, and that . . . I dreaded. Tonight was no different. After about fifteen minutes of just sitting, I finally drove off, stopped by the bank and started my journey to the one place that should have offered me comfort and rest. On the contrary, my home was filled with memories that only made me depressed or angry. As soon as I rounded the corner onto my cul-de-sac, a familiar fog of sadness hovered over me. I eased my car into the garage right beside Cade's gold Infinity, which I never drove, but promised it to Caryn once she got her license. My watch reflected it was now nine-thirty, so the kids had probably gone to bed, at least CJ anyway.

"I'm home," I announced, entering the kitchen and dropping my keys on the counter. Neither of my children responded. The smell of burned hamburger meat filled my nostrils, drawing my attention to the stove, which showcased a dirty frying pan surrounded by splattered grease. A bag of potato chips lay open on the table, and two plates, painted with ketchup and sprinkled with bread crumbs and seasoning salt, marked the places where they'd both sat and eaten in the breakfast nook. "What is so hard about cleaning up behind yourself," I mumbled under my breath as I lifted the dishes, took them to the sink and rinsed them both in a spray of hot water. While I had the water running, I went on to clean up the mess Caryn had left in her dinner preparation. I couldn't complain too much; after all, she did make sure that they ate. Still, I couldn't help but be a little frustrated.

I finished the kitchen a half hour later, dragged my weary bones upstairs, peeked in the kids' rooms, then drew myself a hot bath. "Mmm," I moaned as I submerged myself into the water softened and scented by a handful of lavender and chamomile bath salts. Will Downing's rich, mellow voice circulated the bathroom, serenading me with soothing lyrics. My eyes fluttered closed and I enjoyed peace for only a few minutes before Will started singing "When You Need Me," along with Chanté Moore, a song meant for comfort, but only reminded me of how lonely I was. Ultimately I knew Cade couldn't have really controlled how long he got to stay here, but God could've, right? I mean, He was still at the helm of the universe, holding things together, making decisions, allowing things to happen, or blocking the hands of the enemy, wasn't He?

"Why did you take Cade, Lord?" I whispered. If I weren't so tired, I would have shouted it at Him, since I wasn't really asking more than I was fussing. I stared through the skylight Cade had installed above the tub so that we could bathe in the moonlight. The stars had the nerve to be twinkling, as if God were winking at me. *You play too much,* I thought. I was scared to actually speak those words out of my mouth, although I knew my very thoughts were no secret to God. I was just tired of trying to figure out what kind of love He had for me to take something away that I loved.

When I had posed that question to my pastor, right after Cade's death, he gave me some stupid answer about God shedding tears over the death of his Son killed by the hands of angry and jealous men. Where in the world did he get that mess from? I ain't never read where God cried. Jesus mighta wept, but even then, He was crying because the people around Him were crying—not because He had a loved one snatched away.

"Pastor Blake, I need you to show me in the Bible where it says God cried at Jesus' death, or anywhere else for that matter, because I ain't never read it. Not only that, but Jesus said that no man could take His life, but He laid it down and could take it up again. So what reason would God have to cry when as soon as Jesus gave up the ghost, He was right up there with Him? When did God experience losing someone that He would never see again?" I felt my face getting hotter as I let tears stream from my eye sockets. "If I had the chance of seeing Cade again, I think I could hold back some of my tears."

"And you can see him again, Sister. In the sweeeeet by and by," he answered, throwing up one hand and looking toward heaven. "Glory to God!"

I narrowed my eyes into slits, angry at Pastor Blake's insensitivity. He was going home to a pair of thick brown thighs in his bed, while I was going home to cold sheets on top of a mattress Cade died on. Wasn't there some kind of bereavement-etiquette class pastors were supposed to take in seminary or something? If so, he must have opted not to take it. His words were no more comforting than a bed made of needles and nails. "You have a nice day," I snarled, turning away from him abruptly.

"Let me at least pray for you 'fore you go," he called after me, but I kept a steady stride to my car, where the kids were already waiting, hopped inside and screeched away.

I didn't want prayer. I didn't want people patting on my back and asking how I was "holding up." I didn't want to hear that I'd see Cade again in the "sweet by and by" if I lived right. And since that seemed to be all the people at my church had to offer, I decided not to go anymore.

The first few Sundays, it felt weird not being in a place of worship, holding up my hands and singing psalms and hymns, but I made myself feel better by tuning my television to inspirational networks and watching program after broadcasted program of Dr. Frederick K. C. Price, Kenneth Copeland, Joyce Meyer, Creflo Dollar, Felton Hawkins, Joel Osteen and T. D. Jakes. Now, if I couldn't get the word from all of them put together, there was no word to be gotten! A few times when the TV ministers tried to emphasize about "forsaking the assembly" or, in other words, attending church by TV instead of in person, it only took an instant for me to decide that I'd watched enough ministry for the day and turn the channel. But then it seemed that every Sunday, between the seven of them, one of them was always inviting me to an upcoming service. I got sick of that, so I stopped watching altogether and started spending my Sunday's prepping for the store's revamp.


Now business was booming, and I was in the store every single Sunday. To increase my Sunday revenue and drive more traffic to the store, I'd implemented a Sunday-brunch corner, serving small croissants filled with various meats, cheeses, chicken or tuna salad or just butter, along with a featured flavored coffee from Aromas, a small nearby coffee shop. In exchange for featuring their coffee, they allowed me to place flyers and coupons in their store every week, committing to give them to every paying customer. Even with a later opening and earlier closing, I was almost doing more volume on Sundays than I did on two weekdays combined, and even got requests from local book clubs in my area to host a few meetings there.

Oh yes! Sweet Jream's was quickly evolving into the place to be on a Sunday afternoon, which reminded me, as I still sat amidst a tub of slowly disappearing bubbles, of my full day coming in just a few short hours. Before I could think through the next day's outlook, my thoughts were interrupted.

*"I love you enough to keep asking you to come to my house, to come visit me."*

I turned my head away, trying not to listen. In doing so, my eyes fell upon a page torn from one of CJ's coloring books. "What was he doing in my bathroom?" I asked out loud, determined not to hear God. "I'ma get that boy tomorrow. He know he doesn't have any business being in my room." CJ had neatly stayed within the thick black lines that imaged Pepé Le Pew tightly holding on to, and planting kisses upon, a female cat frantically trying to get away. My talking aloud to myself wasn't enough to silence God.

*"I love you just like that, Jream. Even though you're fighting, trying to get away from me, I love you enough to not let you go."*

# Chapter 2

"I'm getting married!" Tweet announced as soon as she walked in for work.

"What!" we all shrieked, and rushed toward her as if we were all playing the Super Bowl. Her hand was already positioned high in the air for us to admire the sparkling diamond her boyfriend of 2½ years—now fiancé—had given her the night before.

"How did he propose?" Shanice asked, twisting Tweet's hand back and forth to get a view of the ring from all sides.

"Oh, my goodness! It was soooo romantic," she cooed. "On the beach, with the water washing over our feet, just before the sun went down." Her right hand rested over her heart as she gazed at the ceiling, remembering her moment of bliss. "There was a live band playing 'You Are So Beautiful' in the background, and we were walking along, picking up shells and presenting them to each other. Then he was like—'Oooh! Look at that one right there.' He ran ahead of me and stooped down, acting like he was picking up another shell. When I got to him, I was like, 'Let me see.' He turned around on one knee, with the ring in his hand, and he proposed!"

"Awww! That is so sweet!" Shanice exclaimed. "It was better than the proposal I got."

"Which was what?" I dared ask.

"It was some raggedy 'We ain't getting no younger, we might as well do this' proposal, like that Jagged Edge song," she said, rolling her eyes and dismissing the memory with a quick flick of her hand. "How you gonna propose like, 'Hey, I don't have nothing else to do.' But I like a dummy said yes. My nose was so wide open, I didn't have the sense to make the man go talk to my daddy or get down on his knee or at least ask me over a lobster-and-steak dinner."

"Do you regret it?" Tweet asked, mesmerized by the glimmers of light reflecting off the facets of her ring.

"Girl, no. Aaron has been the best thing that's ever happened to me. He could have just proposed a little better." Shanice chuckled. "We'll be married twelve years in July and it's not always been fun, but it's always been heaven."

"Yeah. I know what you mean," I said, instantly reflecting on my marriage to Cade. Our time together had been wonderful, but just too short-lived, even though it had been almost twenty years. Reading my thoughts, Tweet rubbed a comforting hand across my back.

"'Better to have loved and lost than to have never loved at all,'" Taylor commented. "Because my love life is like the desert—dry!" We all burst into laughter.

"Chile, I'm tryna get out of this mess I'm in,"

Michetta confessed; then without warning, she burst into tears, catching us all by surprise. Our eyes shot around nervously to each other for a few seconds; then Shanice stepped in and wrapped her arms around Michetta. Tweet and I stood silently for a full minute, unsure if we should move or not but ready to listen.

"LaVeil is cheating on me," she blubbered. No one spoke a word for the next few seconds. I couldn't think of a single thing to say.

"Are you sure?" Tweet finally spoke. Michetta bobbed her head quickly.

"Yeah," she whispered. "I'm sure. I found condoms."

"Mmph!" Shanice moaned, and shook her head slowly. "How long have you known?"

"For a while." Michetta shrugged. "I should have listened to my mom. She told me I was too young to be getting married, but you know when you get eighteen, cain't nobody tell you nothing."

"We all make mistakes, Michetta. The important thing is that you learn and grow from them. Have you talked to him about it?"

"Yes, we got into a big fight last night and he asked for a divorce!" She was bawling. "I love that man and I've been faithful to him. I don't deserve this!" Tweet disappeared for a few seconds, then returned with a handful of tissues. "Thanks," Michetta said before blowing her nose and trying to compose herself. Shanice remained at her side with her arm draped around her shoulders. "I'm sorry, y'all. I'm sorry, Tweet—guess I kinda put a damper on your announcement."

"It's okay. We all need a shoulder to cry on."

"Do you need to go home?" I offered.

"No, I need to be here, where I don't even have to think about it." She sniffed loudly as she dabbed at her eyes. "I'll be all right."

"Do you know what you're going to do?" Tweet asked.

"Not yet. I don't know whether to fight for my marriage or just let him go."

"Well, try not to make any rash, emotional decisions," Shanice advised. "Those are the ones we usually regret."

Michetta nodded her head quickly. "I'll be all right. Excuse me." Still wiping her eyes, she went to the ladies' room.

"That's just a shame," Tweet commented sadly. "I don't know what I'd do if that were me."

When Michetta came back, it was like nothing had ever happened. "So, have you set a date?" Miraculously, she looked totally refreshed and pleasant. Eager to share her joy, Tweet didn't hesitate to answer.

"Yes! Next year on September sixth." She glowed. "I can't wait!" Tweet babbled on about her wedding dreams and initial planning thoughts. "Can I have my bridal shower here?"

"Of course," I readily agreed. "What you need to ask is can you have that day off, because you know if you're in the store, I might try to make you work," I teased as I walked into the back room to complete a stack of paperwork and sort through the mail.

I'd been working on combing through my new insurance policy for the store, which was taking me forever, since there was so much red tape. I had marked the policy off in sections, reviewing segments of it daily, making notes and jotting questions. Honestly, I just need a few minutes to finish it but that's a few minutes I didn't have. Grudgingly, I spent the next two hours working through more sections, but was relieved that I would be done reviewing the entire document in another day or so. Needing a break, I rose to my feet, stretched and dawdled to the coffee-maker to pour myself a cup of energy, then moseyed out to the sales area.

The store was buzzing with customers who casually and comfortably browsed through merchandise, pinning items up against their bodies and making purchasing decisions. With my mug in my hand, I circled around to my customers.

"You ladies finding everything okay?" I beamed.

"Yes. This store is really nice!" the woman commented. "And I am just loving these slippers! I've never been in here before, but I tell you what. I'ma stop going to Victoria's Secret! They too high anyway for something you gon' have on for all of five minutes."

"But his reaction is worth it, isn't it?" I nodded, encouraging them to continue shopping. "Let me know if I can help you find anything."

I spotted Michetta over in a corner sitting on the floor, carefully positioning some bras in a cabinet. "You feeling okay?" I asked, squatting down.

"Oh yeah." She waved her hand. "I'm fine. I'm not gonna do but one or two things—die or keep on living, and I don't think this is gonna be the thing that will take me outta here. I'll be okay."

"Let me know if you need anything," I said, standing to walk off.

"I might need some time off to visit a lawyer," she threw in, stopping me in my tracks.

I eased back down beside her and began helping by lifting the bras out of the box and removing the plastic packaging. "Do you think you've given it enough thought?" I asked, trying to be objective. She answered with a shrug.

"Don't nobody want nobody who don't want them." I couldn't refute that point. "I mean, we all wanna be loved, we all wanna feel special and chosen," she added, biting into her bottom lip. "So when someone says to you, 'I don't love you anymore,' and 'I don't want you,' is there really anything to think about? If I want the marriage, but he doesn't, what good is that?"

"Well, I think you have to at least consider his emotional state when he said whatever he's said. Could it have been said in the heat of the moment? I mean, have you two really sat down and talked about the status and health of your relationship?"

"He's cheating on me, Jream!" she exclaimed, smudging away tears the second they escaped from her eyes. "Do you know what that feels like? Do you know how much less of a woman I feel, knowing that I couldn't keep my husband from straying into another woman's arms? From between her legs?" she asked, beginning to wail. "Do you know how miserable it is to have your husband climb into your bed in the wee hours of the morning—if at all—knowing he just climbed out of another woman's bed? Knowing that the same sexual pleasure you two used to share, he's now sharing with someone else? Do you know what it's like to lean over to kiss your husband's lips and smell the scent of another woman all over his face?" Anger took over her expression.

I knew all of the questions were rhetorical, so I just listened, but the truth of the matter was, I couldn't identify with anything she'd just said. To my knowledge, Cade had always been faithful to me.

"It's hell, Jream! It feels just like hell," she stated adamantly. "I know this doesn't compare to death, and I don't mean to sound cruel and insensitive, but at least you know where your husband is laying at night . . . and right now I wish LaVeil was dead." She finished staring blankly at a bra she held in her hands. "I'll be right back." She leapt to her feet and rushed for the bathroom, but a customer had it tied up, so she shot to the back.

As I sat there, finishing up the bras, I thought about her heartache and pain and how it compared to mine. I realized that we both had been devastated. Just a few minutes ago, I thought that death was the ultimate stab in the heart, but now, having heard her plight, I wasn't so sure anymore. Was a husband sleeping in a grave better than a husband sleeping around town? I don't know that I would have been able to deal with Cade not coming home at night while being with someone else.

"Is Michetta all right?" Tweet asked, walking up behind me.

"I think she'll be okay."

"She should just leave that joker. That's what I would do," she added, admiring her ring. "Life is too short to spend it with someone who doesn't really love you."

"Yeah, I guess it is. Life is just short anyway, I think."

"I'm going to do my best to live mine to the fullest. If Alonzo doesn't wanna live it with me, I'll leave him in the dust."

"Well, judging from that rock that's blinding everyone this morning, it looks like he wants to live the rest of his life with you, so I don't think you have to worry about that." I chuckled, reaching for her hand again.

"Yeah, you're right. He loves me!" she declared as she bashfully drew her shoulders up to her ears, with a wide smile. "And I love him too!"

"Love is hard to find, so make sure you hold on to it," I stated, becoming a little teary-eyed myself.

# Chapter 3

Next Sunday, I awoke early and lay in bed, just staring at the colored page I'd taken to bed with me a week before. The more I looked at it, the more I ran out of reasons not to try to go to church that morning. As silly as it was, I even tried to convince myself that I had a stomachache . . . or a headache . . . or I felt the onset of menstrual cramps, but none of it was actually true. "All right, all right!" I huffed out loud, overriding my desire to stay as far away from a steeple as I could. As soon as I thought Tweet was up, I picked up the phone and dialed her number.

"Hello," she answered after three rings, sounding as if she was already up.

"Good morning, I need a huge favor."

"Yeah, I can tell, because you're calling on a Sunday morning. What's wrong?"

"Do you have plans today? I need you to open up the store for me. I'm not going to be able to make it in today."

"Is everything okay?"

"Yeah. I just need to take care of something that I've been putting off for a while."

"I really wasn't planning on doing anything besides catching up on some reading and doing a little cleaning but both of those could wait. I'll open the store for you."

"I would appreciate it."

"No problem."

I lay there for another fifteen minutes before finally pulling myself from bed. After a few minutes of yoga stretches, I padded to the closet and looked through my church clothes section to find something to wear, quickly settling on a Calvin Klein black dress suit trimmed in satin and black satin trimmed pumps to match. With that out of the way, I began to hum a tune to myself, feeling more encouraged than I'd had in months as I glided down the steps and into the kitchen. With a rattle of some frying pans, a griddle and my mixer, it wasn't long before the delicious aroma of cinnamon-battered sourdough bread stuffed with bananas and orange date compote, scrambled cheese eggs and chicken apple sausage wafted upstairs, tickled Caryn's and CJ's noses and enticed them from their sleep. Caryn made it down first, still in a pajama shorts set that was about a half-inch away from having her behind exposed. She still had a scarf tied around her full head of bendable rollers.

"We're having company?" she asked suspiciously as her eyes jumped from one serving platter to another.

"Nooo," I sang jubilantly. "Just wanted to enjoy breakfast with my children."

"But, Mom, this is breakfast on a whole 'nother level." She grabbed a plate from the cabinet and began piling on food. "Normally, when you eat with us, you have a Nutri-Grain bar and a cup of coffee. We haven't had a breakfast like this since . . ." Her voice trailed off, but I knew the end of the sentence. Neither of us spoke for a few seconds. The silence was only interrupted by the sound of my fork scraping out the last bit of eggs from the pan.

"Well, I'm trying to do a little better. Can you pour some juice, please, and ask your brother to come down?" Caryn huffed just low enough that I wouldn't say anything as she set her plate down, went back to the cabinet and got three glasses.

"CJ! Come eat!" she hollered. Well, that was one way to do it.

I set the platters on the table and poured myself some coffee while Caryn placed two other plates down, for me and her brother, then grabbed forks and knives.

"Good morning, Mommy," CJ said brightly. "I brushed my teeth already, see!" He exposed as many of his twenty teeth as he could, then glanced at the table. "Wow! It looks like a restaurant in here! You cooked this?" he asked in disbelief.

"Yes, and what's with you two that I can't cook breakfast without you both thinking something's going on."

"Because you don't hardly *ever* cook. You used to cook a lot when Daddy was still alive, but you don't anymore." And there it was. Caryn looked over at me and I saw *That's exactly what I was going to say* scroll past her eyeballs, like text on a marquee. "Caryn just normally fixes me a bowl of cereal," he finished without stopping.

I gulped down a mouthful of guilt and chased it with a swig of coffee before I spoke again. "Well, I'm giving your sister a day off." Caryn plopped into a chair and picked her fork up to start digging in, but I stopped her. "Let's say grace first."

Her eyebrows shot up in surprise as she shrugged. "Okay."

"I wanna say it," CJ offered as he held his hands out toward us to grab. I nodded, giving him the go-ahead. "Thank you, Lord, for the food we eat and fresh clean water that we drink. Thank you, Lord, for rest and care and little children everywhere. And thank you for letting Mommy stay home and have breakfast with us and that I don't have to have cereal today. But thank you for letting Caryn take care of me when Mommy is busy."

*Where did this little boy get all this prayer power from?* I wondered as I felt the stabs of how busy I'd become that my children were actually shocked that I'd cooked a simple—well, maybe not too simple—meal. We ate breakfast while the gospel artist Smokie Norful sang through the small Bose system, which sat on the kitchen counter.

Caryn began singing along in a voice I hadn't even realized she had. The lyrics fell out of her mouth casually, but they held such richness and power, the girl brought tears to my eyes right there at the table. I had to excuse myself to run to the bathroom and pull it together, not just because she sounded so incredible, but the lyrics poked at my soul. Afraid to look at my reflection, I turned my back to the mirror and sat on the edge of the sink as I dabbed my eyes. I did have a lot to be grateful for.

As the three of us cleared the table, I let them know that I'd be going to church that day rather than to the shop. "I'll be back right after service is over. I'm not going to go to the shop at all today," I announced.

"Whaaat?" Caryn drew out. "You're actually taking a day off?"

"Yep. Don't you think I deserve one?"

"You just never take one, that's all."

"When did you start singing like that?" I asked, not wanting to hear another thing about what I never did, like cook or stay home.

Caryn smiled a bit and hunched her shoulders as she ran a sinkful of dishwater without being asked. "I don't know. I just opened up my mouth one day, and that's what came out."

"She sings all the time, Mom. Sometimes I want her to shut up for a little while."

"Why don't you shut up!" she ordered. "With your big head!"

"All right, you two. That's enough," I injected, stopping the banter before it had gotten started good. "Anyway, I'll be back after church is over. Next week we're all going together, so be ready."

It took me close to an hour, a jar of superhold gel, and a hard-bristled brush to get my hair in some kind of presentable order. I'd brushed edges until my head was sore and still looked like a trip to my hairdresser would have done me some good. I wasn't going to let that stop me from going to church, though. As I pulled on my panty hose, it snagged on a broken nail, sending a run from my waist down to my heel. I ripped them off and decided to go bare-legged, with a pair of open-toed stilettos instead of my pumps. I looked high and low for my Bible and finally found it hidden under a stack of *Essence* magazines by my bedside. "At least it's not dusty," I mumbled to myself, then headed out the door.

Not wanting to go to my own church—in order to avoid the stares and questions I was sure I'd get for being gone so long—I picked a very large church where I could easily get lost in the crowd. I arrived thirty minutes before the service was scheduled to start and was glad to find that the organist was already in place and playing a medley of hymns that had begun to seep into my soul. I watched others shuffle in and begin to get seated, some talking quietly while others spoke quiet words of praise. I had to admit, it felt good to be in church again.

With my eyes closed, I found myself on the verge of tears as I sang the lyrics to "Sweet Hour of Prayer" from the church's hymnal.

"'In seasons of distress and grief, my soul has often found relief and . . .'" I had begun whispering the words aloud when I heard a woman's voice.

"Excuse me." She tapped my shoulder lightly, bringing me out of what was beginning to turn into worship.

I looked up into the smiling and overly made-up face of a heavyset woman dressed in a copper taffeta-and-lace skirt suit with large gold buttons. Copper-

and-gold-colored sequined pumps covered her feet and were accompanied by the matching clutch purse. Not a single hair on her head was out of place, even though it was easy to see that it was a wig or freshly done weave. Beside her stood a man wearing a suit that coordinated perfectly with her outfit. He held a metallic gold handkerchief in his hand, folded into a neat square, and dabbed at his brow every two seconds. Four children—two boys and two girls—trailed behind him, also neatly outfitted in copper and gold, the boys in suits and the girls in elaborate poofy dresses, with gold tights and black patent leather shoes.

"Sure," I answered, maneuvering my knees to the side to allow her and her family enough room to pass in front of me.

"No, no, no, sweetie. I mean, you're sitting in our seats," she informed me with a hint of arrogance as she batted her heavily mascaraed lashes.

I absolutely hated when someone called me "sweetie." To me, "sweetie" was a term of endearment for a five-year-old child, or at least a person's own children. I was neither, so I took offense at both the term and her condescending tone and cringed slightly. "I'm sorry?"

"Sweetie, do you not know who we are? Do you know how much property we own in this and the neighboring seven cities? Didn't you see our names posted on the side of this pew?" She took a step back and read to me the engraved gold plate. "'Mr. Alberto and Dr. Genevieve E. Fauntleroy—Platinum Contributors 2004 to 2008.' You're going to have to move, dear," she stated with finality.

My head swiveled around like the top of a bar stool and I glanced at my surroundings. Was I at church or at a concert with assigned seating? "Excuse me?"

"I *said*"—she emphasized the word "said"— "you are going to have to move." She began patting her foot as she folded her arms across her chest and stared straight ahead. "Devil, I rebuke you right now, you not gone mess my spirit up. I *will* be in my rightful place today!" she declared, becoming more boisterous with each word.

"You can't be serious," I questioned, looking back and forth between her and her husband's faces. She only cleared her throat and continued to wait. My eyes darted around, looking to see who was watching this mini fiasco unfold. I saw a few seemingly disgusted faces, which seemed to say, "That's a shame," expressed by rolling eyes or shaking heads. Nonetheless, no one—not an usher, minister, associate pastor, senior pastor or lay member—came over to ask either of us to consider sitting somewhere else. Coincidentally, we both spoke the exact same words at the exact same time, which forced our eyes to meet.

"You see this, right, Lord?"

After a few seconds of staring, I finally gathered my things to move.

"Thank you, Lord! You're a faithful God," she had the audacity to say. "Did you see her, Alberto? She didn't even have the class and womanly grace to put a pair of stockings on! I'm going to have to talk to the board of trustees about who they let in this sanctuary!

After all, this is the house of God." It was apparent that she'd wanted me to hear her comment.

Instead of journeying to another seat, I let my feet take me straight out the door. Needless to say, the next Sunday, and the Sunday after that, and the Sunday after that, found me at Sweet Jream's from open to close.

# Chapter 4

Taylor was late for work again. I shook my head as I reviewed her attendance record for the past three months. It reflected a string of tardies, call-ins and even a couple of no-call no-shows that had been documented by Michetta. Overall, she was a good employee and a great sales associate, but she just couldn't get herself together to come to work on time. I'd tried to be lenient and give the girl a break, since she was finishing up her last year in college, but still there was no way I could continue to ignore what was before me.

Closing Taylor's file, I moved on to the financial books, carefully reviewing line after line of sales figures and recorded bank deposits. The sales numbers were still trending upward, and with the Christmas season well on its way and Valentine's Day following, things could only get better. Before I could finish tracking my projections and breaking out sales goals by month, week, day and sales associates, the back doorbell chimed, signaling that the UPS driver had arrived with the day's merchandise shipment. I was expecting twenty-three boxes filled with garments for a floor setup change that I'd planned for the next week.

"Good morning," I spoke rhetorically, anxious to get back to my paperwork. I'd barely even looked out the door, expecting to see Yolanda, the usual driver, but instead, I was startled by a voice that sounded as if it belonged to Barack Obama.

"Good morning to you." Quickly my head whipped back around and looked into the eyes of a man who could be easily mistaken for Omar Epps's twin brother. He chuckled a bit at my expression, which probably looked a lot like a deer in headlights. "The other driver resigned, so I've taken over this route," he explained. "I'm Jaxon."

"Oh. Nice to meet you," I said with little feeling to cover my slight spark of interest that seemed to have come from nowhere. "I'm Jream Colton. I own the store." Quickly we shook hands and my fingers instantly sensed warmth and power in his touch. "How many do you have?" I asked, referring to the box count. He confirmed exactly what I was expecting, then began to stack the boxes against a back wall while I pretended to busy myself with my duties. However, I couldn't help but watch him. He worked quickly and steadily while I discreetly absorbed his physique, a well-built, solid frame, standing around six-two, "All right," he uttered, setting the last box on top of three others. "That's the last one." He handed me the electronic clipboard and stylus for my signature, which I scribbled quickly. "What's your last name again?" he asked, with his eyes pointed downward as he keyed in a few numbers. "C-Colton," I stuttered, imagining for a moment that he would program that bit of information in his memory bank. If he did, nothing about his nonverbal language gave indication of it.

"Thanks. You have a great day," he said almost as nonchalantly as I'd initially greeted him.

"You too." Secretly, I hoped he would look up from his clipboard one last time to give our eyes a chance to connect, but no such luck. Like a rabbit, he hopped into his truck and, with a loud rumble, pulled away, leaving me standing in the doorway like we were lovers who were being forced to separate because of a long journey that he couldn't avoid. Catching myself, although it was probably too late, I stepped back inside my store.

"Get a hold of yourself, Jream," I chided aloud. Just then, Taylor burst through the swinging door, shrugging out of her coat.

"Sorry I'm late," she huffed. "I got caught up at school. Our lab time ran over." Avoiding eye contact with me, she hung her coat up and stuffed her purse into a locker. "All this stuff came today?"

"Yeah. I don't want it out on the floor until next Monday. You can go ahead and start prepping it, though. How did things go last night?"

"Pretty good. We had a rush right before we closed. A group of women came in here, shopping for a bridal shower, and picked up practically everything in the store. They took it off the hanger, turned it inside out, then put them down just any old where, like they never heard of putting stuff back where you found it. We were in here for almost an hour trying to get the store back straight. The good part was they spent close to a thousand dollars."

"Great. Had they shopped here before?"

"A couple of them mentioned coming in before and eyeing a few things."

"Well, we could always stand to increase our customer base." I flipped through a rack of garments that had been placed on layaway, checking the names and dates to make sure they were all current. "Before you start on this shipment, make sure that Michetta doesn't need any help on the sales floor. I'll be out there in about thirty more minutes."

"All right. Let me run in the ladies' room real quick and I'll be right out there."

Pushing through the garments, I took note of a long-sleeved sheer red robe trimmed in chandelle feathers and rhinestones, and a matching pair of open-crotch panties. I owned one just like it and it had been one of Cade's favorite things to see me in. Without warning, a flood of emotions washed over me, but I successfully held back my tears. I just didn't feel like it today and I was going to do everything in my power to distract myself from reminiscing about times gone by.

"Be right back." Taylor had cut into my thoughts as she moved swiftly from the employees-only bathroom to the door that led to the sales floor.

"You know what, don't worry about it. I'll work through the stock shipment."

"You sure? I don't mind."

"Positive," I assured her. Although I'd been cooped up in the back room for at least two hours managing my back office, I knew an additional hour or so of solitude would do me good.

When Taylor headed for the sales floor, my tears fell anyway—completely against my will. I missed Cade terribly and I was sick of it. Here I was working like a maniac to keep Sweet Jream's alive and thriving, while he was taking his ease in Zion, sipping virgin piña coladas out of some golden goblet, chumming it up with the Lord in paradise. We were supposed to be running this store together. Not me alone stressing over inventory, work hours, underperforming employees, plus occasional merchandise shrinkage and money shortages. It just wasn't fair. The more I stared at that robe—wallowing in my feelings of desertion and extreme loss—the angrier I got all over again. I became so angry that suddenly I felt empowered as I realized that while I'd been functioning, I'd been living in a gloomy, depressive fog for over a year now.

"That's it," I declared. "You left me, and I'm going to live my life. I'm not going to cry another day over your dead body, Cade Aramis Colton." I thought back to the woman who'd called the morning radio show that morning several weeks back. She hadn't stopped living just because her husband had. As a matter of fact, she sounded like she was living it up.

Grabbing my purse, I shuffled to the bathroom and looked myself square in the eye. I had bags and dark circles under my eyes, my skin was beginning to sag around my cheekbones from all the weight I'd lost, my collarbones protruded as if I were a starving citizen of a Third World country, and my clothes just hung on my body and were no better shaped than if

they were still on the hanger and waiting to be purchased. My hair was brittle and scraggly-looking
and seemed to be thinning at my temples. The whole
perimeter of my head was full of what Martin
Lawrence would call "beady beads." Suddenly I was
ashamed of myself. I'd let myself go so much that I
looked like I had one foot in the grave and the other
on a banana peel. No wonder that woman at the
church said she was gonna talk to somebody about
the people that came up in their church. How was it
that I'd not noticed how bad I looked before now?
And to think that I actually wanted the UPS man to
take a second look at me; it's a good thing he didn't.
I decided right then and there, I wasn't going to live
another day looking like death.

Rushing from the back room, I whizzed past
Michetta and Taylor, rambling off instructions.
"Taylor, go ahead and start on the stock. Michetta,
have Tweet close up without me tonight. I need to
go take care of a few things. Call me on my cell if
you need to."

Both ladies' faces expressed confusion, surprised
by my sudden and unexplained departure. "Is everything okay?" Michetta called after me, but I didn't
stop my stride to say anything more than "Yeah,
everything's fine." At that, I was gone.

Settling into the driver's seat, I turned the key,
barely noticing the low purr of the C-Class Mer-
cedes as it started up and I thought about what it
was I wanted to do first. A massage, have my brows
waxed, get a manicure and pedicure, get some new
clothes—something that actually fit me now that I
was twenty pounds lighter, and definitely do some-

thing to this head of mine, which was far beyond out of control. It had been so long since I'd gotten my hair done, I had no clue as to where to go. I was strangely prompted to run my fingers through my hair, but my fingertips were met by a tangled mess of naps more than two inches thick. It was a wonder I didn't cut myself.

Maybe I could find somewhere to have it braided. Before I could talk myself out of it, I pulled out my iPhone and did a search on African braid shops. Fifteen minutes later, I'd spoken to a stylist named Isha, who, after asking me a few questions about my hair, promised to have me looking like a queen in about six hours. Right away, I headed for East Little Creek Road, equipped with the three latest issues of *O* magazine, which were stuffed in the bottom of an oversized tote bag that never seemed to leave my car.

Isha took one look at my hair and instantly began to reprimand me.

"You should take better care of your hair," she said with a rich and beautiful accent as she pushed her fingers through my mane. "Your hair is very dry. What do you use for conditioner?" I was embarrassed that I didn't have an acceptable answer, although a million different hair products took up space in the cabinet beneath my bathroom sink. I'd tried everything, from Suave to Dark and Lovely to Wal-Mart's Equate brand, but had stuck to no one particular product.

"It, uh—it just depends," I stuttered, hoping she would let me get by with that.

"I will take care of you," she said, both assuring and relieving me. "You will be beautiful."

Settling in her chair, I put my mind at ease and began reading my magazine, flipping randomly through a few pages. The very first words I read hit me like a ton of bricks forcing me to take a deep, hard look at myself and what I'd become . . . or what I really was. Oprah's words were that you get to know who you really are in a crisis. Still turned toward the mirror, I was compelled to stare at my reflection, assessing myself all over again, realizing what my own personal crisis had revealed about me. My crisis showed me that I was a hermit and a hag. I'd totally neglected myself in an attempt to ignore and run from my problems, spending countless and unnecessary hours at work, doing what I could have easily delegated to my staff. My kids had been living off a combination of fast food and frozen, processed meals, plus the meager (and sometimes awful) renderings of a sixteen-year-old cook. Sure, my business had grown, but what about me? My kids? My life and my self-preservation? Water filled my eyes and threatened to tumble from my lower lids, but I pressed the back of my hands against them, coaxing the tears to change directions. Isha noticed my struggle.

"Do I pull too hard?" she asked, concerned for my comfort.

"No, no, I'm fine. Just my allergies," I lied. Lied . . . that is was I'd done to myself for the past several months. I'd lied that I was okay, and things were fine. I'd lied that my kids were getting older and didn't need me as much. I'd lied and said that I looked just fine and outward appearances didn't count for a hill of beans. I'd lied to myself and said that the operation of the store was the most important thing in my life. It was the salve I thought I needed to soothe my hurts, but I'd done nothing but deceive myself. Now, acutely aware of this, I realized it was time for a new truth to be revealed.

"Caryn and CJ," I called out as soon as I stepped foot in the house. As usual, I could hear CJ beginning his anxious descent down the staircase having heard me come in. Caryn, on the other hand, always kept herself preoccupied with the telephone, her iPod or something else that made noise, claiming she never heard me, but I knew that in most cases she was just ignoring me.

CJ hit the landing at the bottom of the stairs with a thud, then rounded the corner to greet me with a hug, but he stopped dead in his tracks at the new woman that stood before him. My hair alone made me look like a totally different person, but the arched brows, fitted jeans and T-shirt I'd picked up and put on after leaving the braid shop had stripped me of at least ten years.

"Mom?" he questioned with what was very close to disbelief.

"What do you think?" I grinned, spinning twice in full circles.

"You look *beautiful*!" In an instant, he wrapped his arms around my neck as I knelt down to his level. He stroked his fingers through the shiny, narrow braids that hung to my waist. "Your hair is so soft and it smells good too," he commented further.

"Thanks, babe." I pressed my lips to his cheek. "Where's your sister?"

"In her room."

"Go get her. I'm taking you two out for dinner tonight."

"Can we go to McDonald's?" He beamed as he held up crossed fingers on both hands. Ronald had really brainwashed these kids.

"Not this time, CJ. I want us to have a real meal for a change."

"But McDonald's is real, Mom," he protested. "Plus, they have the new *Transformers* toy this week and it's one that I don't have yet."

"Maybe we can go on Saturday, but not tonight." CJ groaned for a second but then bounded up the steps, calling out to the teenager of the house.

"Caryn! Come look at Mom! She has some new hair and she said come on, because she's taking us out to dinner," he yelled at the top of his lungs.

I took my shopping bags to my room and began hanging up my garments I'd purchased for my new look, while waiting for my daughter to make an appearance. Pulling out jeans that were cut low in the waist and would accentuate my figure, a few pencil skirts with higher hemlines than what I was accustomed to and even a couple of knit dresses made partially out of spandex, I felt like a high-school kid who was just about to start the fall semester. Pulling my closet door shut, with me still inside, I turned slowly in front of my full-length mirror that hung inside the door, taking note of my curves, although smaller and less pronounced than they used to be. What a difference a change of clothes made. Remembering the days of my youth, I strutted to the back wall with my best catwalk stroll, turned sharply, ending in a hip-thrusting pose. *Man, I looked good!* I looked so good, that for a moment I let my imagination just run free.

*"Jream," Tyra said, standing before me, tall and stately, "you faced some pretty hard challenges this week, but we couldn't find a trace of it on a single photo. Even through your pain, you still found the strength to let your beauty shine through." She whipped out a photo and presented it to me. "You are still in the running to being America's Next Top—"*

"Mom!" CJ called from the doorway of my bedroom, startling me. "We're ready!" I giggled in spite of myself. Then my giggle turned into a chuckle, then into full-blown laughter as I leaned against the door frame. "Mom, you're in the closet?" CJ asked in a tone and octave that really asked, "What in the world?"

"I'm coming!" I snickered as I quickly finished hanging up my clothes. Whipping my head to the side to remove a few braids out of my face, I emerged from my closet, finding my two babies sitting on my bed. Caryn's usual somber and despondent expression changed right away when she saw me. She stood to her feet, with bright eyes and a smile to match, and inspected me from head to toe.

"Mom, you look amazing! Who did your hair?"

"I went to the African braid shop."

"What else did you do to yourself?" she questioned in awe.

"I just had some pampering done today. It was high time—don't you think?"

"Yeah, 'cause you had really let yourself go,

Mom," she added, gathering my hair in her hands, then allowing the strands to cascade through her fingers. *What? Ouch!* "You really look great."

"I'm glad you like it. You hungry?"

"Yes. CJ said you were taking us out. I'm glad about that because I'm tired of cooking."

*Ouch again! The truth hurts.* "I'm sorry, sweetie. But I appreciate everything you've done over the past few months. I'll tell you what, why don't you pick the restaurant tonight. Where would you like to go?"

"Outback," she squealed.

"Outback, it is." I wrapped my arms around my daughter for the first time since I could remember. "I love you, Caryn." Caryn was silent, although she did tighten her arms around me slightly. Realizing that she was not going to give me a verbal response, I switched gears. "Well, let's get going, you two."

"Are those new jeans?" Caryn asked, leading the way to the front door, eyeing the $149 boot-cut retro denim I had on. CJ scampered along the floor, pushing a toy replica of a monster truck.

"Yeah, I picked them up today from Bebe."

"You didn't work today?"

"Only for a little while." My mind shot back to the UPS guy and the way he looked at me, or, better yet, the way he hadn't looked at me. "I had to go do something with myself."

"Can we go shopping tomorrow?" she threw in.

"Sure." I lifted my cell phone, which hadn't been on all day, and my keys from the foyer table. As soon as I switched my phone on, it began to repeatedly chime, indicating unplayed voice mail messages, finally stopping at fifteen. Before I could navigate my way through the functions to listen to all the messages, the phone buzzed in my hand. The number from the store flashed on the display screen. I contemplated whether or not I should answer, then quickly concluded that I should, since I did tell the girls to call me if they needed me, but then made myself unavailable all day.

"Hello?" I saw Caryn roll her eyes as I answered. She hurried her steps toward the car, now more anxious to get out of my presence.

"It's about time you answered the phone!" Michetta yelled. "We didn't know what had happened to you. Are you all right?"

"I'm great. How are things at the store?"

"Fine. I was just getting ready to lock up. We did pretty well today, but there was one issue."

"Tell me about it later. The kids and I are headed out to dinner."

"Where are y'all going? I can join you after I'm done here."

"No, it's just me and the kids tonight, hon. I'll catch up with you ladies tomorrow," I ended as I plopped down in the driver's seat.

"So who's coming with us *this* time?" Caryn huffed.

I was getting a little wearied of her huffing and puffing. "No one."

"Seriously?"

"Seriously," I confirmed. "I just want to be with you two tonight. Is that okay with you?"

"That's fine. I'm just surprised, that's all."

"What about me wanting to have dinner with my children surprises you, Caryn?"

She turned her head and shrugged her shoulders. "I don't know. You just always doing something else, or spending time with other people."

Okay, that was Caryn's third little prick. What was it—beat-up-on-Mom day or something? I bit my tongue, because I'd already come to the realization that I really hadn't spent much quality time with my kids. But still, it hurt to hear it.

We rode the twenty minutes to the restaurant in near silence. Not because I didn't try to get the kids to talk; CJ was preoccupied with his Nintendo DS and had earphone buds planted firmly in his ears, and the few questions I asked Caryn about school, or just her life in general, were answered dismissively with quick grunts and shrugs; then her cell phone rang.

"Hey . . . nothing, just going to dinner with my mom and brother . . . yeah!" She giggled. "I know, right?" I cut my eyes over at her, trying to read between the lines. "I don't know. I'll tell you about it tomorrow . . . yeah. All right. Bye."

"What was that all about?" I asked, trying to sound more conversational than prying.

"Nothing." She began thumbing in a text message, then flipped the phone closed, dropped it into her purse and remained tacit. I held back a sigh, reasoning with myself about how I could break a few barriers that had obviously been put up without me taking prior notice.

"You know what? I think I'm going to start taking one day off per week to spend with you guys," I attempted.

"For real?" Caryn rhetorically and expressionlessly asked. It was a sign of her disbelief. Which I couldn't really be mad about, because the truth was I had indeed made that proclamation two other times before and, regrettably, never followed through.

"Yeah. I need to be at home a little more and see what's going on with you two."

"So you're staying home to spy?" she asked defensively as she whipped her head around, which should have set off some kind of internal alarm for me, but I was feeling so guilty, I started stammering instead.

"Well, no . . . not to spy . . . I just—I just haven't been around much lately, and I need to be." I felt like a kid who had been caught doing something she didn't have any business being involved in. For the rest of the ride, I tried to recall when was the last time I had honestly spent some solid quality time with the kids. My hands began to tremble at the wheel, as I realized that it had been far too long. There had only been a couple of nights shortly after Cade's funeral that we all sat on the couch in silence, staring at the television screen, both of them nestled beneath my arms on each side of me. I pretended to watch a couple of movies, but in actuality, my mind had been a million miles away.

The kids hadn't spoken a word to me about how they felt about their father's passing, and I'd been too selfishly tied into my own hurts to ask them how they were doing. That, and it didn't seem like simply asking them how they were would accomplish anything anyway, so I had convinced myself, as the days passed, that they were okay. Hurt, but okay. After all—they seemed to be acting okay, their grades were fine and there had been almost no changes in their daily behavior. Yeah, they were okay.

* * *

When we walked into the restaurant, I took notice of the smiles I received, especially from men, which made me feel like a million bucks. A few ladies commented on my hair, and, in turn, I tossed my head proudly as I dug through my purse to hand them Isha's business card. Once we were seated, I ordered Aussie cheese fries as an appetizer for us to share, then opened the menu options to whatever the kids had a taste for. "The sky's the limit," I said with a smile, hoping that the conversation over dinner would go better than it had during the ride in the car. CJ asked for chicken fingers and broccoli with cheese sauce, while Caryn tried to test me by ordering the rack of lamb, a salad and a baked sweet potato, then asked the server for a strawberry daiquiri before cutting her eyes at me.

"Virgin please," she threw in before either I or the server could comment. She wasn't crazy.

I found myself struggling for words as we waited on our meals, shocked that I'd been so out of contact with my children that I really couldn't find any words to say. When had it gotten like this? I was actually relieved when Caryn's cell rang out again. She wasted no time in answering it, sliding out of the booth and switching away to the bathroom. I shook my head, feeling mixed emotions that teetered between anger—at her borderline disrespect—and disappointment in myself for letting our relationship suffer to this degree.

While Caryn was gone, CJ and I delved into

the fries and took turns playing tic-tac-toe on his children's menu.

"So how was work today, Mommy?" CJ asked, sounding like an adult.

"Work was . . . okay. I didn't really do much today at the store. How was school?"

"Fine. We got to do an experiment where we dropped Mentos into a bottle of Pepsi and it exploded!" he said, his eyes stretched wide with excitement.

"Really?"

"Yep! And soda went everywhere!" He lifted both hands in the air, splaying his fingers wildly.

"That sounds like lots of fun." I nodded as I popped a fry in my mouth.

"It was. And then when I got home, Caryn's boyfriend came over and gave me five dollars." This time it was my eyes that became widened as I watched CJ fish through his pocket to pull out the money he'd been given by a boyfriend—whom I didn't know my daughter had. He showed me the bill, which he'd folded neatly into a square. "He told me I could have five dollars every time he came over—if I didn't tell you that he was over there."

*What!* "So how much money do you have?" I asked, careful to hide my rising anger, not wanting to put CJ on alert.

"I got about"—he pressed a finger to his chin, crinkled his brows and looked up at the ceiling— "maybe ten thousand dollars or something like that." I couldn't help but chuckle, but at the same time, if CJ thought he had close to ten grand, he must have had several dollar bills saved up. That meant this boy, whoever he was, had been over way too many times for me not to know about it.

"So, do you like him?"

"He's okay. He always gives me money, so I think I do like him. Plus, he gives me extra money if I don't bother him and Caryn when they are in her room or your room," he ended as he stuffed the money back into his pocket. This time I couldn't help but gasp, sputter and cough as I felt a truckload of bricks tumble onto my head and shoulders. I grabbed for my glass of iced tea as Caryn slid back into the booth.

"Dag, Ma! You spittin' all over the food," she said, crinkling her nose. My eyes became piercing as I stared at her incredulously. "Are you all right?"

"I'm fine," I spoke deliberately after a few gulps of my beverage. "Why don't you tell me what all you did today."

"I ain't do nothing," she answered just as the server brought our food. It looked and smelled delicious, but my appetite was spoiled. I stopped talking just long enough for our meals to be set down on the table.

"What exactly does nothing consist of, Caryn?"

She shrugged as she spoke. "Went to school, came home, did my homework, met CJ at the bus stop and helped him with his math."

"That's it, huh?"

"Yep." She cut into her lamb, then forked a piece in her mouth after dipping it in a pool of Cabernet sauce. "Mmm," she moaned. "This is so good!" While I knew she was referencing the food, I couldn't help but think about her making that same noise with her legs spread open as some little boy stabbed inside her body, calling himself "sexing her up." I couldn't even think straight—let alone enjoy my almost $30 double-lobster-tail meal. "What about your day?"

I cleared my throat as I tried to clear my thoughts, and at the same time make some split-second decisions. "I've decided to take some time away from the store," I announced, not even giving that thought a chance to circulate through my entire brain. Caryn's eyes popped wide open.

"For real? Why?"

"I told you on the way over here, I need to spend more time with you two," I answered without looking at her. Instead, I focused intently on melting the rounded blob of butter on my potato.

"But what about your store, Mom? Who's going to take care of that?" She furrowed her brows, feigning concern.

"I'll have the ladies at the store run things. I can manage some things from home."

"How soon are you going to do that?" She nervously picked up her daiquiri and brought it to her lips. I fought back the temptation to slap it out of her hand, but I would have had to slap myself first for allowing her to order it in the first place. Suppose she was drinking behind my back? Yeah—I definitely had to take a leave from the store and handle my business at home.

"Right away."

"Yay!" CJ yelled. "Then you can help me build stuff with my Legos!"

Caryn's response wasn't so accepting. "Isn't it

going to take you some time to get everything straight before you stop going?"

"Nope. Things are in pretty good shape actually. You know I've been there just about every day from open to close for the longest time." My tone was exacting enough for disappointment to begin to settle onto Caryn's face. "Now it's time for me to get things straight at home, which I should have been doing all along. Don't you think?" Caryn could only nod, then excused herself to the bathroom once more, making sure she took her cell phone with her.

*Yeah, make sure you tell that boy that playtime is over!*

By the time I got home with my now boxed food, my head was booming with a full-blown headache. I directed CJ to the bathtub, Caryn headed straight for her bedroom after blurting a quick and unfeeling "thanks for dinner out" and I went to my home office. I logged on and started firing off e-mails and planning a meeting with my management team.

I already took great care of my employees, but I knew I would have to offer some raises, since I'd be increasing tasks and responsibilities. The store was doing well, and raises were definitely doable. I was sure I could get them to manage the store more closely and without so much oversight on my part.

It would take me the better part of a week to get things lined up to take some time off. I carefully and evenly divided the store's major processes and procedures between my key holders, and revised a few things in my standard operational procedures manual. I decided that I'd still make merchandise purchasing selections from home and would actually work in the store only one or two days a week during school hours.

Thinking of school, I jotted a note to myself to make sure that school was where Caryn was spending her time during the day. My stomach did another flip at the thought of my baby girl being sexually active . . . and in my bed at that. Finished in the office, I stood to my feet, stretched and headed for my bedroom after stopping by the linen closet for fresh sheets. I wondered how many times had I come in from work, exhausted, and fell asleep on top of the nasty, dried-up, wet mess they'd made. That alone made me want to burst into Caryn's room and go upside her head, but I knew I had to be a little more strategic in how I handled the situation.

Completely repulsed, I not only changed my bedclothes, but I tussled for a good fifteen minutes with flipping my mattress, breaking out into a full sweat. I wasn't even sexing on it anymore, and I'd be doggone if I let my sixteen-year-old daughter wear my mattress out.

# Chapter 5

"Look at Jream!" Tweet screamed as soon as I entered the store the next morning. "What did you do, get an extreme makeover? Coming in here, looking all sexy!" Right away she got Michetta's and Shanice's attention with her exclamations. They both looked up from behind the cash wrap area where they were going through the opening procedures of verifying the cash on hand, stocking bag and boxes for the day and recording sales figures from the previous day's operation.

"Jream, is that you?" Michetta squinted her eyes in jest. "Because if it's not, I'm about to call the cops on this woman walking up in your store like she owns the place!" The opening crew burst into laughter as I strutted my stuff across the sales floor, did a Naomi Campbell turn, did five vogue poses, then strutted back to the door.

Despite the revelation and my restless sleep from the night before, I still felt good, and I had to give it to myself—I looked good too. I'd pinned my braids up, short of a few curled strands at the nape of my neck, dressed my face in minerals makeup and a sheer lip gloss, which gave me an incredibly glowing and radiant complexion, and was outfitted in a black cable-knit above-the-knee sweater dress, which caressed my curves in all the right places, completed by fishnet panty hose and knee-length black boots. I had even taken the time to clean my jewelry, which now gleamed like it had just left the pampered environment of the Tiffany and Company glass case. This definitely wasn't the Jream they were accustomed to. Even I had to get used to the new me.

"We're opening the store an hour late this morning. Coincidentally, the three of you"—I nodded toward my would be newly appointed managers—"are here this morning, which is perfect, because I need to have an emergency meeting, so I'm treating you all to a continental breakfast this morning."

"Continental? Why can't we get some real breakfast? Some bacon and eggs and pancakes, grits, toast, sausage and waffles?" Tweet asked with twisted lips. "There's a Cracker Barrel right up the street."

"It's either pancakes and bacon and waffles, or coffee, Danishes and raises. I'll let you choose."

"Raises? Oh snap! Forget everything that I just said." She giggled.

"As soon as you ladies finish that up, meet me around the corner at the coffee shop," I said with a knowing smile.

As my heels clicked against the pavement, taking me down the block, I saw the UPS truck pulling around to the back side of the building. For a split second, I wished that I were at the store to greet the driver at my back door, but I snapped back to my senses as a car horn blared at me, followed by a catcall.

"Lookin' good, baby," a man old enough to be my grandfather yelled out the passenger side of his car. It had been a while, so I couldn't deny that it felt good to be complimented in some form, even though I wasn't after negative male attention.

By the time the trio made it to the coffee shop, I'd ordered flavored coffees for each of us and an assortment of freshly baked, scrumptious-looking pastries. I'd placed copies of my agenda, along with a designated-tasks sheet, out on the table, plus three individual envelopes holding my raise offering for the manager and both assistants.

"Still, that man is fine!" Shanice exclaimed to the other two as they made their way over to the corner, where I waited for them. "Jream, I can only work mornings from now on so that I can let the UPS man in every day!"

"Is that right?" I responded rhetorically, punctuating it with a chuckle.

"Have you seen him?" Tweet asked.

"Yeah, I met him yesterday." I displayed my lack of interest with a dismissive wave.

"Ain't he cute?" Shanice asked, looking for confirmation of her own opinion.

"He's all right, I guess" is what tumbled out of my mouth, but in my mind, I shrieked, *Yes, he is!* "Anyway, have a seat so we can get down to business." The ladies took a seat and glanced over their agendas while I talked.

Although taken aback, my managers sat in the rounded booth with crossed legs, sipped, nibbled and gave supportive looks and nods while I explained my immediate partial leave and their added responsibilities.

"It's just so sudden, though," Michetta commented once she'd absorbed the news. "One minute you're in the back room, working like a madwoman, and the next minute you've transformed into this totally new, sexy brick house and are leaving the store."

"I'm not going to be far, let's not forget that I do own the place. I just need some time for me."

"It's a man, ain't it?" Tweet threw in, narrowing her eyes suspiciously.

"No!" I said that a little louder than I needed or wanted to, and surprised myself when I realized that my arms had instinctively covered my chest as if my breasts were exposed.

"Okay, calm down! I just asked," Tweet replied, making me even more aware of my unintentional overreaction. "I should have known better than that anyway. We're just wondering what all this sexiness is about all of a sudden."

My mouthful of coffee was only halfway down my throat and was nearly spit all over the table as I blushed with laughter. "Come on, y'all. You all know that a makeover was well overdue and needed. As much as I preach about maintaining a sophisticated and sexy image for the store, you shouldn't be too surprised. Instead of sophisticated and sexy, I had turned into sad and sorry!"

"Well, you're looking supersnazzy and sassy today," Michetta tagged on.

"Thanks. I feel like all of that today and I almost caught me a little boyfriend on the way down here,"

I bragged, puckering my lips and rolling my eyes for a few seconds, bringing out a few snorted giggles from my crew. "But, anyway, I did mention to you raises, which are all sealed in the envelopes before you. I think you will all be pleased with your proposed increases. If not, you can come see me individually and we can discuss it further." I watched the expression of each of the ladies as they opened and unfolded their proposal letters, and watched each of their faces light up like Christmas trees.

"I might just pick up the breakfast tab myself!" Shanice beamed, placing her letter back in its envelope before stuffing it into her purse. "When does this go into effect?"

"Today, since it's the first day of the new pay period. If you are accepting, I'll process the change today."

"Oh, I definitely accept!" Michetta injected, followed by positive responses from the other two women.

"Great! With that said, I think we're all done here," I concluded, beginning to clear the table. "I'll be in the store for a little bit today, but after this, you ladies will see less and less of me for a little while."

"I, for one, am going to start following you and see exactly who it is that will be seeing more and more of you!" Tweet teased.

"Oh, I can answer that one easily . . . my kids!" I pressed my lips together and shook my head, thinking about my grown-tailed daughter. "Momma's gonna be spending a whole lot of time at home."

"And we'll take good care of the store while you're away," Michetta promised.

"There is one more thing that I want to address before we leave." A quick glance at my watch disclosed there were only ten minutes left until I wanted the store to be open. What I had to say wouldn't take long. "There's been an increased amount of shortages and merchandise shrinkage." My face had become stern and my tone unwavering. "I've not been able to get to the bottom of it yet, but I will indeed have my eye on it, and I need you ladies to do the same. When someone steals from the company, they steal from every single one of the employees. Shortages mean less raises, less hours, smaller employee discounts and decreased benefits, just for starters." I stared for a few seconds into each pair of eyes communicating my seriousness. "Now, I will be watching the figures and activities daily, and holding you all accountable for what takes place on the shifts that you're managing."

"What do you mean by that?" Tweet questioned, knitting her brows with an almost offended countenance.

"What I mean by that is although you guys are great to me, responsibility for whatever happens in this store while I'm away, good or bad, rests squarely on your shoulders." There was a tension-filled pause while my last sentence settled in their minds. "If there is a problem, find it and fix it before I get to it."

"I don't think it's fair to get into trouble if we are not the one's guilty," Tweet countered.

"If you're in a key holder position, it's completely fair. It's your ship while you're at the helm. If you can't manage the ship, then I need to reevaluate your role. You're definitely getting paid for it, don't you agree?"

"You get a new look and all of a sudden get grand on us." Tweet's head bobbled around on her neck on the brink of insubordination.

"It's not called getting grand—it's called running a profitable business." Tweet gave no response, but it looked like she rolled her eyes. I made a mental note to keep a sharper eye on her activities. "Any questions, ladies?"

"No," Shanice answered verbally, while the other two gave nonverbal responses.

"All right then. Meeting adjourned."

Together we walked back to the store, making idle conversation, and somehow got turned back toward the new UPS man.

"He's gonna walk in that back door one day and see me standing there in that new fence-net halter top and G-string we got in yesterday!" Shanice exclaimed, looking over her shoulder and shaking her rump.

"You need to stop that." Michetta giggled. "You're gonna mess around and pick up more than the UPS man!"

"Hey! Oww! Hey!" Shanice sang as she popped her fingers to enhance her dancing.

"What am I going to do with you?" I asked, laughing at her antics.

"Ring me up for this new outfit when we get back inside so I can wear it to work tomorrow."

"And wear it in your casket when Aaron finds out," Tweet added.

"You right about that!" she agreed, laughing.

"Anything I buy is for a private show for my baby, and for my baby only." Shanice stuck her key in the door, letting us all back in the store, although I only entered to turn around and leave.

"All right, ladies, I'll be back in a little bit. I'm going to go take care of a few things."

"That's what you said yesterday, then came in here today looking like new money." Michetta chuckled, flipping the window sign from CLOSED to OPEN.

"And wait until you see what I do next," I teased.

"All right now! Don't hurt nobody!" Tweet screamed as I winked and shut the door behind me.

I got in my car, pulled onto Jefferson Avenue and drove toward Caryn's school. Half of me expected her to be there, while the other half didn't know what to expect. I just seriously hoped to find her in her proper place.

I entered Denbigh High School just as classes were changing, so the hallways were flooded with kids of all shapes and sizes, some of them dressed like they had absolutely no parental guidance at home. But I was a fine one to talk.

Much to my surprise, when I walked into the office, Caryn was sitting there, wearing a scowl on her face, a skirt so short I could practically see the crotch of her underwear and a tight T-shirt that displayed a running faucet that read *Dripping Wet* across the front, accessorized by a pair of bright yellow pumps and jewelry. She was shocked to see me, but I was completely appalled and outraged. The fact that for some reason she'd landed herself in the office was one thing, but the way she was dressed was completely over the top.

"Mom, what are you doing here?"

I stared at Caryn incredulously, my eyes still trying to convince my brain to believe that this was my child. *My* child!

"Where are your clothes? You did not look like that when you left the house this morning." I distinctly remember seeing her in a baby blue velour jogging suit, with some light blue Baby Phat sneakers that she'd begged for.

"I . . . umm . . . I had to . . . they're in my locker because . . . ," she said, fumbling over her words, but I wasn't looking for an explanation.

"You better get your little hot tail up and go get them!" I bellowed, snatching her up by the arm. In my peripheral vision, I saw the school secretary peer over the front counter, then turn her head away. Other students that were in the office snickered, or just plainly laughed out loud. Caryn scuffled to her feet and tugged at the skirt, which didn't budge at all, and rushed past me to exit the office into the hallway.

"Dang! Yo' momma done snatched you up!" Some man-child guffawed at her from behind me. "You betta get them clothes on, shorty!" Angrily I spun around and looked him dead in the eye. "Oh, 'scuse me. My bad." He chuckled under his breath, delivered a stack of papers to a teacher's mailbox, then beat-boxed his way out the door.

"Mrs. Colton, were you coming to sign Caryn out?" the secretary asked, approaching the counter.

"Actually, I was just coming by to make sure that my daughter was here today, and has been here every day. I've recently been made aware of some extracurricular activities she's gotten herself involved in, and wanted to make sure that she's attending classes the way she's supposed to."

"Oh. So you had no idea that she was here waiting to be picked up?"

"No, I didn't. For what reason?"

The secretary turned red in the face as she told me briefly in a whisper that Caryn had been suspended for giving a boy a blow job in the boys' bathroom.

"What!" I shrieked. I opened my mouth again, but I literally could not think of anything to say other than a string of short words that weren't really words at all but sounded like "ut . . . aht . . . et . . . ih," and then a long sigh, *"kuhhhhhhh."* As she handed me a form to sign, the secretary seemed to understand every word I didn't say.

"I'm sorry," she whispered.

Caryn walked back into the office in her jogging suit, looking crazy in the face, knowing that by now I knew. "Little girl, if you come near me, I swear this woman is gonna have to call an ambulance for you and the police department for me. Get to the car! And it might be in your best interest to sit in the back, where I won't be able to reach you!" I spat. Without a word, Caryn spun around and left, while I stood, flabbergasted, ashamed and embarrassed. With my elbows propped on the counter, I rested my head against my hands, feeling the onset of a migraine. The secretary patted my shoulder, then moved down the counter to assist someone who had come into the office. A few minutes later, she returned, finding me stuck in the same position.

"Are you okay?" she asked, or, in other words, "I know you're in shock, but you can't stand here all day."

"No, but while I am here, can I just please review my daughter's attendance record?" My voice was shaky and my hands trembled as if I'd drunk two pots full of black coffee.

"Sure," she responded, trying to convey comfort in her tone. She dug through a file, located an attendance chart and slid it toward me. "Here you are."

I glanced over the card and saw that she was present and accounted for each day. "Well, at least she's not skipping classes," I mumbled, handing the card back.

"I know it's hard to deal with, but can I share something with you?"

"Sure." I sighed and looked up somberly into her eyes as tears trickled from my own.

"I know you're upset, but even our toughest battles somehow make us strong and do us some good," she said, patting my hand.

I pressed my lips tightly together and nodded, respectfully acknowledging what she thought were words of encouragement. *Yeah, right.*


"Have you lost your ever-loving mind?" I screamed, once I got in my car. Wisely, Caryn positioned herself behind the driver's seat, so if I wanted to get a good smack in, I'd have to turn all the way around and reach behind the seat. I knew I couldn't put my hands on her right now and not go to jail, so I resorted to screaming and hollering all the way home instead. I could hear Caryn sniveling behind me as—in anger—I called her every name I could think of besides the "B" word.

"And who is this you've been sneaking in my house?" I bellowed. "And don't even fix your lips to lie to me or I swear to the Lord, Most High and Mighty, that I'ma stop this car and jump in the backseat and beat you silly!" Right then, I had to slam on the brakes to keep from running into the car in front of me, for I'd been focusing on Caryn's face through the rearview mirror, instead of on the road in front of me.

"I—I . . . it's just one of my friends from school, named Erik," she stuttered.

"What are you doing letting him in my house, and even more so in my room and bed?"

"Ma, we weren't in—" Before she could finish her sentence, I swerved like a maniac into a parking lot, jammed the car into park and tried my best to turn my body 180 degrees around to smack her, but I couldn't get a good angle, since she hunched down as far into the floorboards and into the door as she could. With my knees in the seat, I swung around my seat about eight times, slapping her upside her head and blurting words, until I caught a glimpse of the shocked faces of other motorists who were passing by. I composed myself and slumped back in my seat, put the car in gear and drove home, with knitted brows and tightened lips. As we pulled up to the house, I said one more thing to my daughter. "When I stop this car, I'm going to give you one minute to get out and make it safely to your bedroom, where you better stay for the rest of the day and all of tomorrow. If I catch you outside of those four walls, I can't promise you that you won't end up in the hospital." I paused only for a second while she pulled her backpack onto her shoulder. "And give me that cell phone." Without making a sound, she slid her phone into the front passenger seat, then quickly let herself out of the car, rushed across the yard and let herself into the house.

I sat in the car the next hour, lost in a sea of mixed thoughts.

"Lord, have mercy," I uttered, more as an expression than a request. I wanted to pray, but I just couldn't. I didn't have the faith to believe that my words would travel past the roof of my car. Especially since the more I thought about it, the more it became my own fault.

Why didn't I come home more?

Why hadn't I made my children a priority?

Why did I let the communication door close between me and my daughter?

Why wasn't I checking homework, attending PTAs, watching movies, going skating and shopping and out for pizza and having family game night, doing all that stuff that I full well knew a parent was supposed to do to nurture their kids?

Why had I not been more sensitive to their needs?

Why had I been so selfish and neglectful?

*Why?*

Even so, Caryn still owned her own behavior . . .

# Chapter 6

Caryn successfully avoided me for the next two days, and I avoided her. I hadn't quite figured out what it was that I could have said or should say—so what else could I do but keep silent? Since I'd confiscated her phone, I took the liberty of reading every text message that chimed in. Needless to say, I was distraught by the sexually infused messages intended for my daughter:

> wer u at?? got me hard 4 nutin
> u still gon let me get in dem draws 2day
> yo popsicle ready—cum get it
> lemme pop dat cherry 2nite

After a couple of days of that, I had her phone disconnected, although it cost me $500 to break the contract. Next I took a hammer to the handset, slid the broken fragments into a large envelope and slid it under Caryn's door. I was becoming angry all over again.

It didn't matter that the next day, around noon,

while in the shower, I heard God whisper clear instructions to me.

*"Go tell Caryn that you love her."*

I pondered it in my heart for a few seconds, but dismissed it with the thought *That girl knows that I love her.* I transitioned my mind to planning dinner. It had been so long since I'd used my oven, I couldn't be certain that it still worked. I planned to try a new recipe I'd come across for Mediterranean chicken and would add twice-baked potatoes and a garden veggie salad to it. I cringed at the thought of sitting at the table with Caryn and having to actually look at her face, but I couldn't keep the child locked in her room forever.

Exiting my room, I headed for the kitchen and ran right smack into Caryn coming out of the bathroom. She jumped when she saw me although she had nothing to worry about. My urge to hit her dissipated on my way back from dropping CJ at school this morning. "Get dressed; you're going to work today," I snarled. My eyes rolled as she slid into her bedroom and came out minutes later, dressed in all black, with a gold belt, to conform to the dress code. She then took a seat in the living room to wait for me.

When we got to the car, she looked at me nervously before getting into the passenger seat. With a twenty-minute ride ahead of us, I figured now was as good a time as any to confront her about what CJ had shared with me.

"So when exactly were you planning on telling me about your boyfriend?" I asked, keeping my eyes on the road, and as best I could, keeping my tone even and low. Her head whipped around toward me as she fumbled with her seat belt.

"I . . . I was scared to tell you."

"Scared for what reason, Caryn? Because I told you you couldn't have a boyfriend until you turned seventeen?"

"Yes," she whispered.

"So how is it that you have one, when I strictly forbid you to? How is it that you are so willfully disobeying me? And what is your grown tail doing for birth control?" I shot before she could answer questions one and two.

"Mom, I'm not having—"

"Don't you sit up here and lie to my face! Do you think I'm stupid?" I did try to control my emotions, but just like that, at the sound of a lie forming and falling from her lips, my control mechanism was out of whack.

"No," she answered feebly.

"So, I'm going to ask you again. What are you using for birth control, or are you mindless, careless, stupid and irresponsible enough to get pregnant and have a sea of regrets?"

"We've been using condoms," she said lowly, with embarrassment.

"What are you whispering for? You can't be ashamed, 'cause if you had any dignity, you wouldn't have been in the bathroom with some boy's"— I struggled to keep my lips together so that a nasty word wouldn't fly out of my mouth—"penis stuck in your mouth!"

Caryn dropped her head into her hands and began to cry, which made me remorseful about fussing at her a second time. I willed myself silent as we drove the rest of the way to the store. By the time we pulled into the parking lot, she'd dried her tears away, but she couldn't hide her dejected expression.

A huge part of me wanted to wrap my baby in my arms, apologize and comfort her. I wanted to let her cry on my shoulder and tell her it would be okay and we'd get through it, and I would take her to the doctor's to make sure she was okay, or else get her any medicine she needed. But, instead, my hands grappled for my purse and keys, and when my mouth opened, none of that came out. "Get with Michetta when you get inside. She'll tell you what to do. And don't come in here until you get your torn-up face together, but you don't have all day." I headed straight to my back office, leaving Caryn outside as she pulled herself from the car. "Good morning," I blurted to Michetta, but I didn't wait for a response as I moved quickly to the back. "My daughter is going to be working here for the next two weeks, so help her get situated, please." My eyes rolled from the front window to Michetta's face. "Anything you can think of that needs doing that we've been putting off, give it to her. Scrubbing the toilet, the floors, sweeping, mopping, polishing the racks—anything."

"Okay but why is she here? What'd she do?" Michetta followed me toward the back after glancing out the window and seeing Caryn run the heel of her hands across her eyes.

"She got suspended from school a few days ago." Michetta gasped. "For what?"

"I don't even want to talk about it," I said, side-stepping. "Where is Taylor?"

"Late as usual."

"Call her and tell her don't even worry about coming in today." She'd picked the wrong day to be late again. "My daughter needs something to do with her time—she can work here in Taylor's place." The door to the employees-only area swung closed behind me just as Caryn entered the store. I glanced around my back room, looking for tasks that I could assign to Caryn that she would absolutely hate. The floor back there could use a good scrubbing, but for the most part, we kept the store pretty clean. A sigh pushed through my lips. "As long as she stays out of my way."

Turning my focus away from my daughter, I began reviewing the weekly and daily sales reports, satisfied with the upward trending of the store's performance. I'd encouraged my staff to try to sell at least five items to every customer who made a purchase by offering her body product add-ons, clearance panties or panty hose, and we were making great strides there, with an overall items-per-sale at a 4.6. Over the next half hour, I worked through some numbers and ideas, and figured that with a little rearranging of a few add-on products, making them more accessible to my customers' hands would help to get me to the goal.

I rose to my feet and headed for the sales area to start visualizing what I'd wanted to change. Before going out, I peeked through the door, semi hoping to find Caryn in misery. Michetta stood in the cash wrap area, counting money, while Caryn seemed to have found a new friend in her. She was smiling, babbling and trying to demonstrate some dance move she'd picked up from *Dancing with the Stars* as she held a bottle of glass cleaner and a roll of paper towels in her hands. I wanted to burst through the door and blurt, "I told you to work, not play!" But, honestly, it did my heart good to see a smile on her face. Instead, I eased the door shut and went back to doing paperwork, hearing both Caryn and Michetta break out in uncontrolled spurts of laughter every few minutes. I would never let it be known, but the sound of them laughing made me laugh too; yet I resisted the urge to find out what they were having such a hee-haw time about.

A stack of applications sat on my desk waiting for my review, and with Taylor being late again, now was just as good a time as any. I read through résumé after résumé, and paragraph after paragraph, of applicants' previous experiences until one caught my eye. Stephanie Sampson's profile looked pretty impressive with several years of retail management under her belt, a college education and currently employed. I decided to give her a call and do a phone interview and then a face-to-face if the phone portion went well.

"This is Stephanie," she answered after only one ring. Her tone seemed a bit harsh, but it changed immediately after I announced who I was and why I was calling. "Oh yes! I thought you were someone else calling. How are you doing?"

"Great, thanks. Listen, I was reviewing your application here and was wondering if you were still seeking employment. I may have an opportunity at Sweet Jream's that you might find interest in."

"Yes, I am still looking."

"Do you have a few minutes for a phone interview?"

"I sure do," she chirped. We chatted for several minutes, with her answering all of my questions to my liking.

"When might you be available to come in for a sit-down interview?"

"I can come today if you have time."

"Ummm . . ." I glanced down at my watch. "Can you be here by two?"

"How about ten minutes 'til, because to be early is to be on time, to be on time is to be late, and to be late is unacceptable."

*All right now!* I thought. "Ten 'til two sounds great. See you then."

Just as I hung up the phone, the back door chimed. Before I realized it, my hands flew to my head to feel that my hair was in place, and I almost stopped myself from glancing in the mirror and smearing on a coat of clear gloss across my lips . . . almost. "Good morning," I said, pushing the door open and folding my bottom lip into my mouth to suppress a smile.

"How you doing?" he asked, writing on his clipboard.

"Great, thanks. Good to see you again." When I said that, his eyebrows shot up in surprise.

"Umm . . . I don't think we've met," he replied, extending his hand. "I'm Jaxon."

"We've met." I nodded. "I'm Jream Colton, the owner. Remember?"

"Oh yeah, yeah." His head bobbed slowly. "You, uh . . . you changed your hair or something."

"Or something. Come on in," I said with a chuckle. I flung my braids behind me as if I were in a Pantene commercial. "So how's your day going?"

"Pretty good, I can't complain." Jaxon hoisted boxes off his cart and stacked them on the floor.

"I sure could, but I'm striving not to."

"Things are never as bad as they seem," he said, smiling optimistically. I couldn't help but smile back. "The darkest hour is just before dawn."

"You're right, which is why I'm just giving up on complaining," I agreed.

Jaxon checked his clipboard, did a box count and realized one box was missing. "I'll be right back." I watched from the door as he climbed into the back of his truck, then hopped down three minutes later, toting my last package. "Here you go." He stacked the last box on top of another he'd already brought in, then handed me the clipboard for my signature. "All right, you're all set," he added, standing just inside the doorway.

"Thanks," I said, handing the clipboard back to him, then waited for him to clear the threshold so that I could secure the door.

"Oh, one more thing," he added, patting the shirt pocket on his chest. Jaxon plucked out a business card and handed it to me. I glanced down, wondering why he would hand me a generic business card, when I'd had an account with them for years. "Read the back," he said, then jumped into his truck.

Flipping the card on its reverse side, I smiled as I read the handwritten words: *It would be a pleasure and an honor to take you to dinner. Jaxon—555-9247*

*PS: Sorry for rushing off, but I hate face-to-face rejection—*☺

I did have a chance to chuckle a bit before my guilt began to creep in, feeling like I was cheating on Cade, although his body had been cold for a whole year. Trying to dismiss the notion, I dropped the card on my desk and decided to venture out to the sales floor for a few. As soon as I stepped foot out of the back room, the conversation between Caryn and Michetta came to a slow halt and the giggling died down. My eyes bounced back and forth between both of them.

"You didn't have to stop talking just because I came in the room." Even with that said, neither of them said a thing for several seconds.

"Did today's shipment arrive?" Michetta asked, obviously feeling forced to say something.

"Yeah, it did." I unknowingly grinned.

"What's with that big horse grin?"

"Nothing." I shook my head quickly but still wore half a smirk.

"You weren't looking like that a little while ago."

"My day is not allowed to get better?" I looked over at Caryn, who had moved on to rubbing the racks with wax paper, which made the hangers slide more smoothly.

"Sure it is. I just want to know what happened to make it brighten up. It didn't have anything to do with the doorbell I heard a few minutes ago, did it?"

"What would make you say that?" I crinkled my brows, trying to deny it, but it didn't work. Michetta saw right through me.

"Ooh! It did have something to do with the UPS

guy!" As soon as she said it, her hands flew to her mouth, remembering Caryn's presence. "Sorry," she silently mouthed.

"I'm trying to figure out what all the laughing out here was about."

"Nothing really. Caryn and I were just talking about our favorite TV shows, that's all."

"Well, Caryn has been having enough fun. I don't think she needs any extra," I shot back, trying to put my angry face on. "Did she tell you why—" Two ladies entered the shop before I could finish my sentence, but not before Caryn gave me a horrified glance.

"Welcome to Sweet Jream's," Caryn spoke, rushing forward to help the customers and divert my conversation.

"Taylor did call a little while ago, by the way," Michetta continued. "Said she couldn't come in today because she had cramps."

"Yeah, right. A young lady will be coming in for an interview in a couple of hours," I informed Michetta. "I need to start thinking about Taylor's replacement." Michetta's eyebrows shot up. "I need people who can come to work on time. If she can't do it, I can find people who can."

"You're the boss," she stated.

"I sure am."


As promised, Stephanie arrived at the store several minutes before her interview time. After introducing herself from afar, she waltzed around the store, observing things, and seemingly making herself familiar with the merchandise and store layout. I liked that.

I invited her to take a seat on one of the corner sofas while I went to grab her application and résumé, then joined her a minute later. I extended my hand toward her, and right away I detected the strong, unpleasant odor of cigarettes.

"I'm Jream," I started. "Thanks for coming in today."

"Oh, my pleasure!" She smiled brightly as she stood to her feet and shook my hand. I took note that she was professionally dressed in a black-and-gray herringbone pantsuit, with a crisp white blouse beneath her jacket. She pushed a pair of smart-looking wire-framed glasses up the bridge of her nose, then took her seat again.

I asked some standard interview questions, with my nose jumping and twitching the entire time bothered by the smell of her habit. Though tempted to ask her how much she smoked, I knew it wasn't relevant to the interview. The conversation did come up, however, when I reminded her that Sweet Jream's, like other retail stores, was a smoke-free environment.

"Do you have a problem with that?"

"Oh, not at all. I do smoke, but, of course, I would go outside or something," she replied, looking slightly discomfited.

"Or something?" I asked, encouraging her to explain what she meant by that.

"I mean, I'd just go outside on my break."

"Oh, okay." I pressed a smile on my face. "So when would you like to start?"

"A week? I'd like to give my current employer some notice. I hope that won't be a problem."

"No, a week sounds good." I closed the interview and saw her to the door. By then, I was ready to call it a day.

When I went to get my purse from the back, I thought again about Jaxon's dinner invite and smiled to myself. I picked the card up, re-read it, then slipped it into my purse, uncertain of what I would do with it. Maybe I'd give him a call; dinner couldn't hurt, right?

"Let's go, Caryn," I said, coming out of the back room and heading for the front door.

"Mom, can I stay here and work until closing?"

*What's that about?* I thought. It had caught me by surprise. Within a few seconds, I'd gone through a full reasoning process, concluding that if she wanted to work, I had nothing against it.

"Work or play?" I said snidely. "And how are you going to get home?"

"Work. Can you come back and get me, or maybe Miss Michetta can bring me home?"

I looked over at Michetta. "I don't mind bringing her," she offered.

"Hmph! I guess so. Michetta, call me later with the sales numbers."

"Yes, ma'am."

At that, I left, and strangely yet pleasantly, I thought about Jaxon all the way home.

# Chapter 7

I had no plans for my Saturday other than indulging in some self-pampering and relaxation, starting with a cup of steaming coffee flavored with hazelnut creamer. I'd already taken Caryn to the store, where she'd been working every day after school and all day on the weekends. CJ was trampling across the backyard with the boy next door and a football, the two of them making all kinds of noise, leaving me to lounge lazily on my back terrace in a comfortable seventy-two degrees. It was just what I needed.

When I finally had enough calmness stored in my body, I thought back to Monday and talked to my daughter about the behavior that had gotten her suspended. Well, actually, I didn't talk to her about it, I just told her to get dressed and ready to go to the doctor.

"Since you've made the decision to become sexually active, you need to at least be smart and protect yourself." That was about all I said, still having not gotten over what she'd done.

I had the doctor prescribe her a low hormonal dosage of birth control pills, and she had to be treated for chlamydia, but, thankfully, that was the worst of it.

"Don't bring home no babies," I tagged on to my "conversation" with her, and let the rest go.

I should have said more, I know. Something loving and motherly—but I didn't. The more days that passed, the easier it was for me to dismiss saying anything further. Now it was Saturday and the notion was pretty much gone from my mind altogether.

As I lay back on my chaise, I turned to a blank page in my journal, ready to pen some thoughts and track some emotions. I'd had Jaxon's number for two weeks now, although I hadn't seen much of him since he'd given it to me. I had not actually called him either, but I still had his card, and I looked at it every day. Every time I did, self-reproach would creep over me . . . up until about a week ago when it seemed that Cade had sent me a message straight from heaven.

I'd been soaking in the tub, as usual, staring up at the sky and trying to figure out how I was supposed to go on. Really, I was getting a little tired of mourning and promised myself I wouldn't do it anymore, but I guess I didn't know how to stop. I'd thought about Jaxon as I peered through my bathroom door and at my nightstand, which was the resting place for a huge bouquet of pink roses he'd sent to the store that afternoon. Shanice screamed in my ear with excitement when she'd called to tell me he'd dropped them off for me with the store's shipment.

"Oh, you been holding out on us!" she accused. "You lucky I'm married or I would have to fight you over that fine man."

"Stay out of grown folks' business," I teased. "There's nothing going on between us," I commented truthfully.

"Mmm-hmm," she replied in disbelief. "Maybe not today, but something is brewing on the horizon. Y'all been out?"

"No, nosy!"

"It won't be long. It's time for you to get out and start dating again anyway. Especially since you have spent money sexying yourself up. I know you didn't do all that just to be sitting at the house."

"I did it for me, okay? Can't a woman have some self-esteem?"

"I'm just hoping self-esteem turns into some romantic steam."

"I'm not ready yet."

"Why not!" she chastised. "How long you gonna take to get ready? I don't mean to sound cruel, but it's not like your husband is locked up for a few years. Cade is not coming back. You have got to move on."

Her words stung like a switch in the hands of a grandma that didn't play. "You can't talk until you've been in my shoes, Shanice," I'd snapped, becoming irritated.

"Maybe not, but I know you're too young to live like a hermit crab. Now, here is someone who is handsome, got a good job and no kids, who is—"

"How do you know he doesn't have children?"

"Because I asked him, duh!"

"Oh."

"Girl, you better not let this good man slip through your fingers. He sending you flowers and everything and you sitting back thinking of days gone by."

"It's not just that," I argued.

"Then what is it?"

"It's . . . it's." Honestly, I couldn't think of anything.

"That's what I thought. Ain't nothing wrong with him. He's a nice guy. He's interested in you. You need to call him and stop trippin'."

I sighed in defeat. "I'll be by to pick up my flowers."

When I got to the store, the girls, including Stephanie and her smoky self, had twenty questions lined up for me, along with the chant "Jream's got a boyfriend! Jream's got a boyfriend!" which they sung in unison. As I thought more about it that evening, I realized Shanice may have been right. I was trippin'. There was nothing wrong with Jaxon, and though a little afraid to admit it, I was pleased that he'd shown some interest in me. All that evening, I toyed with the idea of giving Jaxon a call. . . . *At least thank him for the beautiful arrangement, if nothing else,* I coached.

It was hours later that I'd convinced myself to reach out to him, although I just couldn't bring myself to call. Instead, I thumbed a text message, counted to three, held my breath and pushed send.

Thank you for the roses. They are beautiful and I appreciate you thinking of me.

In less than a minute, my phone chimed, indicating the arrival of his response.

Beautiful flowers for a beautiful woman. You're welcome.

It felt good. It really did.

The next morning, no sooner than my feet hit the floor, I leaned over to my flowers and inhaled their sweet fragrance. I had to tell myself several times over that I was in no way acting in infidelity. I knew that I wasn't, my heart just had a really hard time believing it.

As I lay back in the tub that evening, I told myself again that I was doing nothing wrong, then reminded myself of the declaration I'd made to live my life. After all, I couldn't make love to a ghost.

"Forgive me, Cade," I whispered up at the skylight. "You know that I've always loved you."

I pulled myself out of the water, patted dry and applied some moisturizer to my skin, then slipped into a pair of silk pajamas, before walking through the house to make sure my doors were secure, and my children were behaving themselves. Caryn lay across her bed, writing in her journal; CJ lay in bed, reading *The Adventures of Captain Underpants*. "Good night," I said to them both, then padded to my bedroom.

Nestling between my own sheets, confident that no one had slept on them but me, I reached for my iPod on my night table. I planted the buds in my ears while my thumb circled the dial to the playlist selection. I did have a specific playlist for relaxing at bedtime, which was a mix of Sade, Rachelle Ferrell and Al Jarreau. By the time those three finished singing lullaby after lullaby, I was generally completely relaxed. Tonight, though, for some reason, I adjusted my Nano to song shuffle, lay back on my pillows and closed my eyes. The very first song that played was one I never even knew I had. It was Eric Benét's "Still With You," which was clearly about a lover gone on and releasing the one he left behind to love again: *Live your life from this day on and love again. I know you'd do the same for me. That's the way that love is supposed to be. . . .*

I replayed the song at least ten times, wiping away tears, and crying for the loss of my and Cade's relationship one last time. When I woke the next morning, I felt something new wake up with me, something I couldn't explain, but I just knew that I was free to love again and would move on.

I jotted these things in my journal as I watched my son play, and toyed with the idea of calling Jaxon, entertaining myself for close to an hour with what I might say, how I thought he'd respond and the possibility of what could be.

"What are you smiling about?" CJ asked, running up to me.

"A new beginning," I said, knowing he wouldn't know what I was talking about.

"What does that mean?"

"Nothing, babe. Do you two want something to drink?"

"Yes, please," they answered in unison.

"Okay, I'll be right back." The boys scooted off momentarily while I, still wearing a smile, slid from the chaise, went into the kitchen and pulled two juice boxes from the refrigerator. I leaned against the counter and looked over at my cell phone, which lay on the countertop with my keys. *I'm calling him,* I decided.

When I picked up the phone, I saw that I already had a text message from Jaxon.

Just wanted to say good morning. Hope you'll have a great day.

I beamed as I absorbed the thoughtfulness of his words and returned the text.

Good morning to you too—my day is fantastic! :-)

Seconds later he replied:

I'd still love to take you to dinner. Are you free tonight?

I wasn't doing a darned thing wrong, but I found myself scared to respond in his favor. I chewed on my bottom lip, trying to figure out how many ways could I be busy, when I actually had nothing to do.

"Mom, may we have something to drink now?" CJ asked, bursting into the kitchen and wiping sweat from his brow. I had forgotten all about the thirsty boys. I mumbled an apology and handed the chilled boxes to CJ, who thanked me and ran back outside with his friend.

Maybe not tonight, but soon, I texted back.

Will you come to church with me tomorrow? I'd be honored.

That made my lips tighten. Church was the last place I wanted to be. I would have rather gone to dinner than to church. But church was safer, I reasoned. A little less personal, although we'd sit right beside each other. And it would be easier to go to a casual lunch after church than a formal dinner date, where I'd have to tell him where I lived and have him pick me up.

Sure. What church and what time—I'll meet you there.

He sent the details, along with a smiley face, and said he looked forward to seeing me, which made me smile again. I looked up at the ceiling and raised one eyebrow.

"No tricks this time, God."


After I threatened Caryn's life and told CJ that he was to tell me if Caryn so much as opened the front door for the mailman (who didn't even deliver on Sundays), I left home to meet Jaxon. When I arrived, I found him waiting in the foyer for me. He had a wide smile spreading across his face as I stepped closer to him.

"Good morning!" he said, leaning in to cordially peck my cheek. "Glad you could come."

"Thanks."

"You're right on time. Praise and worship is just getting ready to start," he added, leading the way through a set of double doors; I trailed a few steps behind. Jaxon walked almost to the very front of the church, then stepped back to let me inside the pew row he'd chosen. Once we were comfortably seated, he began singing and clapping. I, on the other hand, had my guard up for the entire morning service. I thought it had been unnoticeable, but as soon as the last amen was said, Jaxon asked if I was okay.

"I'm fine." I nodded. "Why do you ask?"

"You just seemed so tense the whole time we were there."

*Did I?* "No, I'm fine."

"How'd you enjoy the service?" He gently and barely placed his hand on my back, guiding me through a small crowd of people and into the parking lot.

"It was good," I said, although I really hadn't been paying much attention. My thoughts kept wondering who in the congregation would see me with Jaxon and start the wheels turning in the rumor mill. I must have turned my head a thousand times. Sometimes Jaxon turned to see whom or what I was looking at, but he mostly kept his focus toward the front of the sanctuary, or had his eyes closed and was moving his lips prayerfully.

We walked the rest of the way to my car in silence. I couldn't say what he was thinking, but I was halfway hoping he'd ask me to lunch and halfway hoping he'd let me go home, although I would have been disappointed with the latter. In my mind, I began chanting, *Ask me, ask me, ask me!*

"Thank you for coming with me."

"Thank you for having me."

"So . . . what are you getting ready to do right now?"

I shrugged. "Go home and relax a little bit, I guess." *Ask me, ask me!*

"Well"—his brows lifted with a bit of hesitancy—"would you like to go to lunch?"

*Yes!* "Ummm . . ." I was really struggling, but somehow "Sure" tumbled from my lips. I saw a genuine smile spread across his face, which made me smile, as much as I didn't want to seem desperate or anxious.

"Would you like for me to drive?"

*You don't even know this man,* one side of my brain said. *Take a chance, Jream!* the other side yelled. "That would be nice." My head bobbed with my response.

"I'm parked right over there." He pointed across the lot to a very clean and pristine late-model extended-cab black Chevy Silverado. "I can bring the truck to you, if you don't want to walk," he offered.

"I don't mind walking."

There was a pleasant silence between us as we strolled to his truck, then rode to Virginia Beach's Cheesecake Factory. Other than some old-school Hezekiah Walker and the Love Fellowship Crusade Choir singing about believing they were going to make it, no other voices were heard.

When we arrived at the restaurant, Jaxon was nothing less than a perfect gentleman, letting me out of his truck, walking on the curbside of the sidewalk, pulling out my chair, letting me order first—just everything that I would expect from a respectable date. He impressed me.

"So how'd you get the name Jream?" he asked while we waited on our meals.

"Well, my mom, unfortunately, miscarried her first two babies, and when she delivered me full-term and healthy, she said I was a dream come true. She spelled it with a *J* to make it unique, because she knew there would never be another one like me."

"She's right about that. You are unique." I blushed.

"And there's no one else like you . . . anywhere." He paused momentarily. "But you know what? I think she spelled it with a *J* because she knew one day we'd meet and she wanted our initials to match. Jaxon and Jream." He looked up into the ceiling as though seeing stars. "Doesn't that sound nice?"

I practically spit out my mouthful of tea in an unsuccessful attempt to hold in my laughter. "You act like we're married or something."

He shrugged. "I see something I want, and I'm not afraid to call those things that are to be, not as though they were. That's what the Bible says to do, right?"

He couldn't be serious. I cleared my throat nervously, not knowing how I should respond. Before I had a chance, our server appeared, balancing a tray atop his left hand.

"Here you go, ma'am." He set down a steaming bowl of chicken breast sautéed with fresh mushrooms in a rich Marsala wine sauce served over bow tie pasta. "And for you, sir." Jaxon closed his eyes, inhaled and moaned as he was presented with shrimp and chicken sautéed with onions, tomato and peppers in a spicy Cajun sauce on top of fresh linguini.

After placing my napkin on my lap, I picked up my fork, ready to dig in, but Jaxon stopped me. "Let me bless the table." Oh yeah. He held his hands out across the table for me to take hold of, and once I did, he prayed like he was trying to get folks saved.

"Father, we thank you for this day, and for your unending mercy and grace. Thank you for this meal we're about to receive, and we ask that you would sanctify it and make it nourishing to our bodies as you continue to nourish our spirits. And lastly, I thank you, Lord, for allowing me the extreme pleasure of sharing a meal with an incredible and beautiful woman." My eyes popped open on the latter part of his prayer, but his were closed tightly and sincerely. "In Jesus' name, Amen."

"Wow. I don't think I've ever heard grace said like that before."

"I believe in expressing my gratitude. God's been good to me." He stabbed a piece of chicken and shrimp onto his fork before twirling it through his noodles, then offered it to me. "You like spicy foods?"

"Spicy is okay." I could hardly put my lips around the piquant morsels for smiling so much. "Mmm! This is delicious," I commented, wiping my mouth while he filled his own. "Do you want to try some of this?" I asked, offering him a sample of my dish as well, but instead of feeding him, I forked it onto his plate.

Through mouthfuls of food, we made small talk about the store, his job, my children, and his only sister, Jamillah. I opened up a little about Cade's passing, and he shared that his mom died when he was sixteen. I told him that my parents were in South America serving in the Peace Corps on a twenty-seven-month assignment, and he told me his father was serving time on three 20-year sentences. After hearing that, I fell speechless. He rattled his fingers on the table for a few seconds, then suddenly broke the silence.

"Let's order dessert." He grabbed the menu and began to flip through pages.

"I don't know if I can eat another bite."

"Sure you can. Sunday afternoons are made for desserts," he replied. "Haven't you ever seen *Soul Food*?" he asked, referring to the scenes that projected huge Sunday dinners with varied desserts included. "I could take you to my grandma's house right now and she'd have about fifty cakes lined up on the counter that she baked this morning before she went to Sunday school." I giggled at his exaggeration.

"You know good'n well your grandma didn't bake fifty cakes this morning."

"How much you wanna bet," he asked, leaning across the table with raised eyebrows, jerking one arm back to get his wallet from his back pocket. "I'm telling you, every kind of cake you can imagine, she done made it."

"This morning?" I asked doubtfully.

"Yeah!"

"Fifty of them?"

"Mmm-hmm!"

"Any kind I want?"

"Yep."

"How about a brown-eyed Susan sweet potato cake?" Something I had seen on a recipe Web site.

"Pssh!" he dismissed. "Girl, yeah—every single Sunday. Want me to get you a piece?"

"I sure do."

"You ain't said nothing but a word." At this point, I was giggling intermittently as he pulled out his cell phone and punched in the number and began singing Bill Withers's "Grandma's Hands."

"'Grandma's hands used to hand me a piece of candy,'" he sang in a voice that made me burst even more with laughter. "'Grandma's hands picked . . .' Hey, Grandma, it's Jax." My hand flew to my mouth as my eyes widened. I thought he was just playing with the phone. "Yes, ma'am . . . yes, ma'am. Tell Big Pop I'ma still take care of that when I get there . . . yes, ma'am," he continued. "Hey, Grandma, you make cakes today? . . . You did?" He stuck his tongue out at me from across the table. "I know you do, Grandma, but I just asked anyway. You mighta felt like taking a Sunday off." He chuckled for a few seconds. "You got any, umm . . . Brown-eye . . . umm . . ." He looked up at me. "What was it again?"

"Brown-eyed Susan sweet potato cake," I answered. Jaxon repeated it for his grandmother, and right away I could hear her chatty voice rambling off quick words.

"A brown-eyed who? I ain't never hearda nothing like that. You sure that's a cake? I got some black-eyed peas sittin' on the stove, but I ain't got no brown-eyed cake. I 'on't know if I would even wanna taste that!" she said in about three seconds flat.

"Just ate the last slice, huh?" This time I really laughed out loud—too loud to hear her response. "Yeah, I know that's Big Pop's favorite. I just thought you might have saved me a little corner," Jaxon went on. "Well, I'ma try to get by there one day this week. . . . All right then . . . love you too." As he pressed a button to end his call, he looked at me and shrugged. "If you would have asked just five minutes earlier," he said, snapping his finger, "we would have been on our way to Suffolk so you could get a piece."

"You are a mess!"

He took a deep breath, then let it out, feigning disappointment. "Guess we gonna have to order something here." We decided on a huge serving of delectable layers of vanilla cake and lemon mascarpone cream topped with streusel and served with strawberries and whipped cream. "This was pretty good, but it ain't nothing like my grandma's," he said, shaking his head as he fed me the last bite, causing me to almost spit it out on the table in laughter.

We sat for a few minutes longer while the server processed the check. "Thank you, and you guys have a nice evening," he stated, handing Jaxon a small portfolio that held his credit card and receipt.

"I guess I'd better get back home before my children start to wonder what happened to me," I said, patting my full belly as if I were carrying a baby.

"Yes, let me get you home on time. I wouldn't want your son to have to jack me up for bringing you in too late."

I chuckled at his humor.

As we drove back to the church parking lot, where I'd left my car, the heavens opened up and let out all the water it had been holding back, bucket after bucket. Even so, it didn't dampen the wonderful mood I was in, having been treated like a princess at lunch.

"Thank you so much for lunch," I said, pulling

my purse up on my shoulder as he drove up to my car, placing me on the driver's side.

"No, I have to thank you—the pleasure was all mine." He grinned. "I think I have an umbrella back here on the floor." He reached behind my seat and shuffled around for a few seconds, but he couldn't find one.

"Don't worry about it. I can just hop out and jump right in my car."

"Absolutely not." Jaxon shook his head. "I'll be more than happy to get your door."

"No, don't do that, I don't want you to get wet, and my car's right here. By the time you get out and walk around, I can be in my car."

"Jream, no. I'll get your door. That's what a man does." He said it with such finality, I dared not move but complied. In an instant, he hopped out of his truck, walked around to my side and opened the passenger door, then the driver door to my car. In the 1½ seconds that it took me to get from his vehicle to mine, I was nearly drenched. Jaxon had to be soaked to the bone. He shut my door, patted it twice, then jetted back to the driver's side of his truck. After I pulled out, he tapped his horn twice and drove his separate way.

It had been a perfect date. Even the church part.

Instinctively, I drove to the shop to see how things were going, but more so to gloat about my date. By the time I made it there, the rain had ceased, and although still wet, I felt simply amazing as I stepped out of the car in my sapphire Jones New York sleeveless georgette V-necked dress, paired with pewter shoes. Even if the silk material clung to my legs instead of flowing around my body gracefully and flirting with the wind, like it had done this morning when it was completely dry, I still stepped into the store like a runway model, singing Babyface's *There She Goes*.

"Her eyes, her smile, her skin, her smell, her hair! Her walk, her talk, her ways, her savoir faire . . . there she goes'—ah!"

Stephanie was changing an outfit on a manikin, but she stopped to pop her fingers and sing along, while Shanice just looked with raised eyebrows and said, "Mmmmmmmm! Whose church did you go to today, 'cause you look like your soul been set free!"

"Ohhh, I went to the first church of Jaxon." My lashes fluttered around my eyes as I leaned back against the counter.

"How was it?" Shanice asked.

Michetta rushed over from the dressing room, where she'd been helping a woman with a bra fitting.

"It was pretty good."

"Did you hear anything the preacher said, or were you all caught up in those beautiful brown eyes he has?"

"I saved that part for after church." I winked, with a giggle. The ladies let out a unified whoop and waited for me to continue. "We went to lunch after church. It was no big deal." I shook my head to minimize the outing, but the glow on my face said differently.

"That gleam in your eyes is not saying it was no big deal," Michetta teased.

"Seriously, it was nice. We had a nice time. I think I might see him again."

"Now *that's* what I'm talking about!" Shanice exclaimed.

# Chapter 8

I sat at my desk, trying to complete my payroll for the week, but was greatly distracted by thoughts of Jaxon. I found myself daydreaming about spending time with him. There were no shipments scheduled for arrival today, so I knew I wouldn't see him. I began toying with my cell, wanting to send him a message, but at the same time afraid to act on it. I couldn't think of anything to say anyway. And from what I'd last heard about dating was that a woman should never really let on to the man that she's interested. Nonetheless, for forty minutes, I sat staring at my phone, thumbing in text messages only to erase them before mashing send.

I decided to take a chance with just a simple "good morning" message. Then I added "thanks for a great day yesterday," which changed to "thanks for a great time," which changed to "I enjoyed yesterday," then "lunch was nice," then "church and lunch were nice," then back to simply "good morning." Even then, I was reluctant to send it.

"What could it hurt?" I said aloud. I hadn't

entertained the thought of a relationship since Cade had been gone, and what was wrong with having a friend? And honestly, I had had a pretty good time with Jaxon the day before. It wasn't like I was saying I wanted to get married. Before I could talk myself out of it, I sent the message, then stared at my phone for three minutes, waiting for a reply, second-guessing my action and feeling stupid about sending it in the first place. Suppose that man wasn't thinking about me? And here I had wasted almost an hour on nothing. Disappointed, I tossed the phone into my purse and turned back to my payroll numbers, but couldn't pull away from glancing at my phone every few seconds. I picked it up and made sure that it wasn't on silent or vibrate.

"Jream, can I talk to you for a minute?" Michetta asked, pushing through the back room's door, startling me.

"Sure," I answered, casually laying my phone on the desk, strategically keeping it nearby, just in case it chimed. "What's up?"

Michetta sighed before she began and I prepared myself to hear about something LaVeil had done. "Ummm . . . Caryn and I were talking last night while she was here, and she told me why she got kicked out of school."

"Did she?" I asked rhetorically.

"Yeah. She broke down and started crying, saying that she felt stupid and dirty."

"She should feel stupid and dirty," I snapped. "How did she expect to feel—proud of herself?"

"I just felt really bad for her, seeing her that way. And what about when she has to go back to school next week? You know how mean kids can be. They are going to run her down in the ground."

"And whose fault will that be? She made her bed—she's going to have to lay in it."

"I understand that there are definitely going to be consequences, but if you don't mind me saying, I think she's really going to need you, like, every day when she comes in from school. She needs to know that you are there for her."

"Mmm-hmm," I commented with twisted lips. Just then, my phone chimed. Though anxious, I casually picked the phone up from the desk and read the incoming text.

Good morning to you—thanks for spending the day with me yesterday I couldn't help but smirk.

"That must be Jaxon." Michetta grinned, but I didn't confirm or deny. Instead, I dropped my phone back in my purse and folded my lips inside my mouth.

"Was it him?" she asked again.

"Can you mind your business, please?" That was almost like saying yes.

"I'm just asking. You don't usually get text messages and such. And since when have you started smiling because of a phone call or whatever? Yeah, that was him," she concluded. "I'm glad. I think you two look cute together."

"Yeah, but cute don't make relationships work."

"Pfff! You got *that* right! Nobody was cuter than LaVeil and me, but look at us now," she said, shaking her head. "Let me get back out there and find something to do, because I don't even feel like starting up today." Without another word, she left the back room, fanning at the stinging tears in her eyes.

As soon as she was gone, I re-read Jaxon's text and contemplated sending a response. When I couldn't think of anything intelligent to say, I changed my mind and forced myself to get back to work, and this time stayed on task. I pulled out a stack of store copy receipts and began studying the purchase amounts. Several of them that had Taylor's name tagged as the cashier were for incredibly low amounts, showing a string of discounts applied. One receipt reflected that that customer had picked out approximately eight garments but hadn't even paid $5 for the entire purchase. Not only had a 50 percent employee discount been applied, but individual items had dollar amounts deducted from them. I pulled out a highlighter and began marking every suspicious thing I could find, then called Michetta to the back.

"Take a look at these," I instructed, handing her a fistful of paper strips.

"Oh, my stars," she whispered, studying the first two, then glancing over the remainder of the receipts. "Oh my. This girl is just giving away stuff."

"Get me a copy of the schedules for the past two months so I can see who she's been working with." With twisted lips and slanted eyes, Michetta handed me the receipts, then left the room silently, returning with a binder that held the previous weeks' schedules, then disappeared back to the sales area. I sat at my desk and matched the receipt dates to the schedule, notating on a legal pad who had worked the shifts in which the merchandise was being undersold. Fortunately, for my managers, it was an even mix, showing no one manager conveniently "overlooking" Taylor's practices.

She was as good as fired.

Right at two o'clock, I pulled away and gathered my things to leave. One of the things I promised myself that I'd do while I was on this partial leave was to take a dance class. After researching several online, I found a belly-dancing class not too far from the store, and today was the second session. I'd already missed the first, but I reasoned that I couldn't have missed too much and could probably catch up with a little extra effort. Feeling both intimidated and excited, I jumped in my car, drove the few miles over to the studio and jetted to the bathroom to put on a pair of leggings and a big T-shirt, along with a pair of comfy slouch socks. While in the dressing room, I took the time to examine my figure. Although most people would consider me thin, I shook my head at the looseness of my belly from carrying children. I squeezed and massaged the pliable, stretch-marked mass of skin, jiggled it up and down a bit with my hands, wondering if I could ever get rid of it. If I couldn't, I could at least manipulate it and make it look sexy, I hoped.

When I joined the class, I found that I was the only one there dressed like I should have been at Curves rather than a Middle Eastern dance class. There was a mixture of women of all shapes and sizes and ethnic backgrounds, who all had on long, low-waisted circle skirts and little halter tops showing off nearly flat stomachs, and not a single one of them had the hideous scars of proof that they'd at least once been with child. I'd been rubbing cocoa butter, vitamin E, Mothers Friend, shea butter and everything else on my skin for the past fifteen years, trying to get those lines to go away, but I still had every single one that had formed when I carried Caryn. Right then, I was ready to go, regardless of the money I'd forked over for the class when I registered, but it was too late, I'd been spotted.

"Oh, come on in!" the instructor called from the front of the room. "I'm Tatianna—you must be Jream." She rushed over on tiptoes and grabbed me by my arm. "You're going to have so much fun here, isn't she, ladies?" The other participants beamed and nodded, encouraging me to get right in. But, of course, they would—they could show their stomachs in public. Some of them even had belly rings.

Reluctantly I stayed, taking a spot in the back of the room, feeling embarrassed and out of place. I was sure I wouldn't be coming back.

"One of the things we talked about in our last session is how this pattern of movement is really very beneficial for your bodies," Tatianna stated, floating around the room, switching her hips and making individual eye contact with the participants. "Many people have the misperception that in belly dancing you're only utilizing your stomach muscles, but that is so not true. As you found out, you really had to engage your major muscle groups to do some of these controlled moves, right?" In unison the ladies agreed as they held different parts of their body indicating soreness. "But not only are you getting a full-body workout, but belly dancing also can help alleviate some discomforts associated with common women's issues. Things such as menstrual cramping, fibroids, endometriosis and even some fertility issues." She nodded with raised brows. "So there are a lot of good reasons to shake your bellies, ladies! So let's get started."

Tatianna started the music, which put me right in the mind frame of a man sitting Indian-style, wearing a turban, trying to charm a snake out of a basket. She gave some instructions for us to isolate different muscles and move other muscles and had me practically tied in a knot. "Okay, now tighten your right buttocks muscle, while you lift on that side." *Do what?* I tried for several minutes to get only one side of my butt to move without squeezing the other side, and because I didn't have a skirt on, it was very visible that both my cheeks were rising and falling together, unlike Tatianna said to do. Of course, the other ladies seemed to perform the moves with ease, lifting their hips and arching their foot, dropping back down and twisting their wrists. At one point, I just had to laugh at myself and my struggles to control my muscles. I did manage to get the hang of a couple of the movements, and as I performed them to the music, I began role-playing in my mind, dancing for Jaxon. In my imagination, he was my husband, though . . . especially if he was looking at my stretch marks!

At the end of the hour, however, I found that Tatianna had not lied—I had had a great time. I wasn't sure what I was going to do about exposing my belly, or what I could wear to not be so conspicuous, but what I did know was that I would be coming back.

I felt so empowered and sexy leaving there, I actually picked up the phone and dialed Jaxon's number. In seconds he answered with a huff.

"Hi!" I chirped, realizing that I'd not thought about what I may have wanted to say.

"How are you?" he asked, sounding like he was lifting boxes.

"Pretty good." There was a pause as I struggled to find words. "So what are you doing later?"

"Nothing."

"Oh." I was expecting him to say a little more than that. "Well, I wanted to ask if you would like to come over for dinner tonight." *What? Where did that come from?*

"I'd love to have a home-cooked meal made by you. You are going to cook, right?" Jaxon chuckled. "Or are you picking up a bucket of KFC and mixing it with something from that food show *Semi-Homemade*?"

Actually, the latter part of his question sounded like a good idea to me, but I'd stuck my foot in my mouth, so I said, "Oh, I'm cooking." I punched myself in the thigh for that one.

"I can't wait then. What time should I come by?"

"How about . . ." I glanced at my watch, which read 3:05. I would have to go to the store after I figured out what to cook, pick up some food, then get home, prepare it and make sure the house was extra clean. "Seven?"

"Let's make it seven-thirty. I usually get off about six and I don't want to come in my uniform."

"Seven-thirty, it is!" I rattled off my address and ended with "See you then."

Part of me smiled while part of me cursed. And there was a part of me that felt guilty for getting ready to bring another man into the house Cade and

I had shared. Not to mention, I hadn't said anything to the kids about bringing him to the house. I would at least have to mention it to CJ. Caryn would still be at work and I planned on Jaxon being gone by the time she got in.

I rushed to the grocery store, but for the life of me, I could not think of what I was there to get. Circling produce, I picked up a pint of strawberries, with no plans of what I'd do with them. In the canned-good aisle, I picked up rice, corn, French-style green beans and a large can of cream of mushroom soup. Still didn't know what I was cooking. I swung by meats and selected ground beef, chicken wings and a couple of steaks. Did I have onions at home? I jetted back to produce, picked up a large Vidalia onion and a green bell pepper. An angel food cake made it into the basket, along with a carton of eggs, a loaf of potato bread and a half gallon of butter pecan ice cream. Fifty dollars had been spent at checkout and I still didn't have a specific meal plan in mind. The more I thought about it, the better Jaxon's little joke about *Semi-Homemade* sounded. On the way home, I dropped by KFC.

Once home, I put the chicken in a pan, poured the cream of mushroom soup over it and cooked up a pot of rice. Imitation bacon bits were mixed into the pot of green beans, along with a sprinkle of sugar, and I planned to toast a few slices of the bread.

"What's that smell, Mom?" CJ asked as soon as he crossed the threshold. "Something smells delicious!"

"I'm cooking dinner. We're having company tonight," I answered, pecking him on the forehead before taking the stairs, two at a time, to get in the

shower. "Go ahead and get started on your homework."

"Can I have a snack first?" he yelled up the stairs.

"An apple!" His preference was probably cook-
ies, but he'd be all right.

I showered quickly and slipped into a pair of off-
white slacks and a black sleeveless mockT-neck
sweater and slid my feet into a pair of white flip-
flops so I wouldn't look so dressed up. A few swipes
of deodorant went beneath my arms and a spritz of
body spray splashed against my skin. The braids
went up in a ponytail, and I was ready.

Picking up my phone, I made a quick call to the
store to check on things before Jaxon arrived. Caryn
answered.

"Thank you for calling Sweet Jream's. This is
Caryn speaking," she said jubilantly.

"How are things going tonight?" I asked without
greeting her.

"Fine." Her tone became immediately deflated
once she heard my voice.

"Is it busy?"

"A little." A moment of silence hung in the air.
"Did you want something else, Mom?"

"No. Just keeping a thumb on the business."

"Oh."

"I cooked tonight, so there'll be some dinner here
for you when you get off."

"Okay," she said flatly.

"All right, bye."

Things just weren't the same between Caryn and
me since before Cade's death, and even more so since
her little whorish shenanigans. Somehow we just

seemed to have grown apart. I guess in my becoming more and more busy with the store, I hadn't noticed how we spent less and less time together just chatting, sharing hot chocolate or even spending an evening watching television. My eyes just happened to land on a photo that I kept on my dresser of the two of us taken about two years ago. We were at the beach, posing like supermodels, with bright smiles and huge floppy hats. I sighed; those days were long gone.

The sound of the doorbell pulled me away from my thoughts and had me bounding down the stairs. I opened the door for Jaxon, who stood with a small box in his hand.

"Good evening," I said sweetly, but tried not to look too eager, although he looked very nice, dressed in black slacks and a light blue Nike golf polo, which was neatly tucked in at his waist.

"Hi." He wiped his feet on the welcome mat. "For you," he offered, handing me the box.

"I love gifts and surprises," I gushed. "You could give me a bomb in a box, and I'd die with a smile on my face!" Jaxon responded with a hearty chuckle while I lifted the lid of the box to expose a beautiful black-and-gold piano music box that played Chopin's Fantaisie-Impromptu. "Thank you, Jaxon," I whispered.

"You're welcome." He leaned in to kiss me on the cheek, making me blush.

"Are you ready for dinner?" I asked, sheepishly pulling back. He folded his bottom lip into his mouth, looking gingerly at me for several seconds before nodding. "Come on and sit down. The food's ready." Jaxon followed me down the hallway as I gave him a passing-by tour, just pointing out the living room, den, powder room and ended in the dining room.

"Your home is exquisite, just like you," he commented, circling the dining-room table to the far side of the room, then standing by a chair.

"Thanks. Let me get CJ and we can get started." I left him in the dining room, but I returned less than a minute later with CJ beneath my arm. "This is my son, CJ. CJ, this is my friend Jaxon." I caught Jaxon's expression when I called him "my friend," and thought I saw a trace of disappointment. That made me process for a split second what I could have called him so he wouldn't have looked so disheartened. I mean, we weren't boyfriend and girlfriend, were we? We were getting too old for that. What else could I call him?

CJ said the blessing over the meal and we dug in. The mushroom soup over the chicken made it so good I was impressed with myself. I don't know if Jaxon was able to tell it was really KFC, but if he did, he was gracious enough not to say anything. As a matter of fact, all he did say was "This is great, Jream." That is when he could get a word in edgewise, because CJ tried to talk a hole in his head, which was not particularly a bad thing—it took some of the pressure off me to be conversational.

We had transitioned from the dining room into the den and sat comfortably on my tan leather sectional, where we watched Court TV and ate dessert. "Thank you for a delicious meal," he said after downing the last of his ice cream and a cherry-pineapple cobbler I'd thrown together via an instant cobbler mix. I reached for his bowl, standing to my feet to take it into the kitchen.

"Thank you for coming. I hope you enjoyed it."

"I sure did. But more than the food, I enjoyed your company." He paused as he looked up into my eyes like he really wanted to say something. Just as he opened his mouth, CJ darted into the den with a conglomeration of Legos in his hand.

"Jaxon, look what I made!" he shared, dashing past me and toward Jaxon.

"What's that, man?" he asked, giving CJ his full attention. I sauntered to the kitchen while CJ began explaining his artwork in full detail.

"What was he getting ready to say?" I asked myself quietly as I rinsed plates and put them in the dishwasher. I entertained a number of things all centered around "love" or at least "like." When I realized how silly I was being, I laughed at myself. He probably was going to ask if I needed help with the dishes.

CJ was running his mouth full speed ahead, with no signs of running out of words, and Jaxon patiently stayed engaged. He'd taken a seat on the floor and had begun snapping pieces together, making a creation of his own.

"CJ, do you know what time it is?" I asked. He glanced at the clock; then the brightness of his face disappeared as he realized that it was his bedtime. Grudgingly he collected his blocks into a large tub, said good night to us both and left the room. Feeling a bit flirty, I took a seat beside Jaxon on the floor, where he draped his arm around me, pulled me to him and kissed my cheek.

"You're beautiful," he commented. I smiled and he took notice, although he said nothing. "So, will you guys come to church with me this weekend?"

I groaned internally. "I'll need to check my schedule at the store and get back to you." Of course, I planned on later telling him something would be happening that would require my presence. "Can I let you know tomorrow?"

"Yeah," he said, lifting himself to his feet. "That will be fine." He brushed his pants off with his hands, then stretched upward. "I guess I better get out of here. It's getting late." *Okay. I really wasn't expecting that.* He reached his hand toward me to help me off the floor. I stood and walked him to the front door. "Thanks again for dinner."

"You're welcome." Before I could open the door for him, the sound of Caryn sliding her key into the lock caught me by surprise. The knob twisted and she came in, equally caught by surprise at the sight of a man who was not her father standing in our home.

"Hello," she said respectfully, although without feeling.

"Good evening," he responded.

"This is my daughter, Caryn. Caryn, this is Jaxon." I forced a smile on my face, feeling a mixture of disgust and guilt. Disgust that my daughter was having sex; guilt that I'd been caught in the house with my "boyfriend."

"Nice to meet you," she blurted out. "Good night." Jaxon looked a bit surprised, then confused, at her abruptness and probably sensed the awkwardness in the air.

"She just had a long night at work, that's all. And probably still has some studying to do."

He nodded. "Well, let me know about church this weekend."

"I will."

# Chapter 9

Caryn came downstairs in a pair of jeans that were so tight, I was sure that the child had saved them from kindergarten. She'd teamed it with a clingy green-and-white-striped sweater and some chunky green plastic jewelry, plus a pair of white flip-flops. Her eyelids held swipes of green shadow and her lips were shinier than bits of broken mirror lying in the bright sunshine on a busy highway . . . just blinding! She plopped down on the couch with her lips poked out a full two miles in front of her. I couldn't tell if she was upset or just trying not to disturb her lip gloss. At any rate, my frustration immediately shot up.

"Caryn, why in the world are you dressed like that?"

"What's wrong with it? I wore it to school the other day and you didn't say nothing."

"First of all, you aren't going to school—we're going to church. And secondly, I don't recall seeing you wear those too-small pants out of the house, because I definitely would have stopped you."

"These jeans ain't too tight. I got them my size—that's just how they fit," she argued, standing up and spinning in a circle before sitting again, which is how I caught a glimpse of the not-so-hidden thong rising up her back.

"And where did you get those panties from?" My hands were planted firmly on my hips and my lips balled in a knot.

"From the shop! You the one that sells this stuff." *One, two, three, four . . .* , I counted until I got to seventeen.

"Go take 'em off," I ordered through clenched teeth. She popped her lips, stood to her feet and stormed upstairs. Luckily for the both of us, she didn't have to pass me in order to get to the staircase, because I think I might have hurt that girl. "Put on a skirt!" I yelled behind her. "A long one!" I didn't drink, but Caryn had me seriously thinking about starting right that very minute. A hot stream of air slowly left my cheeks through my puckered lips as I stood in one spot and continued counting to fifty.

Just then, CJ came galloping down the stairs with his necktie twisted, shirt hanging from his pants and untied shoes, as if he'd sat through two morning services already and was ready to go to the playground. "How do I look?" He held his short arms out to the side and gave me a toothless grin, proud that he'd dressed himself.

"You look like you got dressed with your eyes closed. Come here."

"Ooh! I'm gonna try that next time!" He grinned, closing his eyes and attempting to feel his way toward me. Silently I moved a few steps out of his path until I caught him peeking.

"Aha! Caught you looking!"

"Mom! You were supposed to stay there," he whined through his giggles. With a few tugs and tucks, I had CJ looking presentable for leaving the house and directed him to sit on the couch. It wasn't long before Caryn returned—in her right mind— wearing a black-yellow-and-white charmeuse dress with satin trim, paired with black open-toed sandals. She'd brushed her hair back into a bun and stuck two hair chopsticks through it, and had stripped herself of the ridiculous makeup that was painted on her face earlier. She actually looked pretty nice. As I parted my lips to compliment her, she showed her nasty little attitude.

"This better?" she sassed with raised brows.

"Caryn, don't make me slap you. It's been a while since I've done it, but I still know how—don't think that I don't." I stared straight into her eyes that seemed to be filled with hatred. "Now you can try me if you want to." She responded by sitting her narrow hips on the seating bench just inside the living room and didn't make another sound.

Jaxon came to get us right on time, decked out in his Sunday best, a black Ralph Lauren Black Label two-button notch suit, a sienna shirt, with a matching tie and double-knot cuff links, and a pair of Allen-Edmonds shoes. Very different from the usual brown uniform slacks and shirt I was accustomed to seeing him wear. I was dressed in a loose-fitting black sheath accented with large black rhinestones, which gave just a hint of my curves underneath, black panty hose, and a pair of Christian Lacroix black satin pumps.

"You look amazing," Jaxon commented as I let him in the front door.

"So do you." I struggled to hide my blush, but it just wouldn't obey my will. "We're ready. Let's go, guys."

"Good morning," Jaxon spoke cordially to the kids.

"What's up, man?" CJ responded in his best teenager impression, slapping his hand into Jaxon's, while Caryn mumbled a quick hello.

"Caryn, you look very nice."

"Thanks," she barely whispered, scooting past him and out the door to his Silverado.

"Thanks for coming with me today," Jaxon said as we walked to his truck.

"Thanks for having me."

"I think you'll enjoy the service." I only nodded in response as he opened the passenger door for me and helped me climb inside.

We arrived at the church, registered CJ into children's church and got seated right before praise and worship started. I felt an unexplained comfort for the first time in a long time. The choir started with Ricky Dillard's "Our Father, You Are Holy," causing several people to stand to their feet, with closed eyes and raised hands. Even Jaxon. I stayed glued to my seat, afraid that if I moved, God would see me, although I did clap my hands just a little.

The music and songs became increasingly faster until the church broke out in a full-blown frenzy. I watched silently as a woman with a crooked curly wig on her head ran back and forth across the front of the church. An usher with a little puff of a pony-tail on the back of her head closely chased the woman with what looked like a folded sheet, ready to cover her hemline if she should happen to do what church folks called "fall out." Other parish-ioners were clapping and hollering words of praise to God.

"Thank you, Jesus!" someone cried on my left.

"Glorrayyy!" came from my right.

"Praise Him, Praise Him," the pastor shouted into the microphone before shuffling into a few steps of his own. "You know God's been good to you! Somma y'all need to give God a breakthrough praise!"

I know that was aimed directly for me, even though I wasn't the only person frozen in place and the pastor didn't even know me. I really wanted to stand up and get involved—wave my arms around, scream at the top of my lungs, holler out "hallelujah"—but my lips were stuck together and my behind was still firmly superglued to my seat. Not only that, but my arms were folded across my chest and welded there. The only thing that was actually moving on me was my foot, which was on a mission to tap a hole through the floor, and my brain couldn't make it stop.

The choir started a reprise of James Hall's "God Is in Control," repeating those words over and over again in harmony and mixed syncopation, which is what got the church in a praise uproar in the first place. Even Caryn shocked me by standing, rock-ing, clapping and singing. When the congregation got to shouting again, my baby girl broke out of the pew and went screaming down the aisle. That was it for me. Immediately I began to weep, but I was careful to stifle my sobs with sealed lips. My tears were burning a hot path down my face and neck, then into my dress, and finally seeping through the crevice between my breasts. I felt Jaxon's hand tap my shoulder slightly, and I looked up to see him handing me his handkerchief, which provoked even more tears. I dabbed at my eyes as I watched Caryn dance and jump until she finally fell to her knees at the altar and cried out to God as if she were pleading for her life. Maybe she was.

A few minutes later, when the church settled a bit, Caryn, with the help of an usher, slowly made her way back to her seat, still sobbing.

"I'm sorry, Mom," she wailed, practically falling in my arms. "I'm sorry." I hugged my baby tightly, nestling her head against my bosom and wetting her hair with my tears. Her arms tightened around me as she shook uncontrollably for the next few minutes, unable to pull herself together.

"I'm sorry too, baby," I whispered.


The service transitioned to the offering and then to the message, but I could hardly concentrate on what the preacher said, because I was so emotionally overwhelmed by Caryn's repentance. I barely stopped crying myself, and even found myself whispering a few words to God.

By the time the service was over, I was completely worn-out. I think Jaxon was scared to say anything to me. He just gently took me by the hand as we left the sanctuary and headed for the children's church area. If it wasn't for Caryn still connected to my right side, I probably would have fallen into Jaxon's arms and let him carry me.

We completed the sign-out procedure and CJ came charging at us with a sheet of blue construction paper that displayed cutout pictures of some biblical story on its front.

"Hey, man," Jaxon greeted.

"Hey, Mr. Jaxon! I had so much fun! We learned that God can talk to you however He wants, even through a donkey!"

"What!" Jaxon humored.

"Yep, 'cause look right here." He held up his sheet of paper. "See right here, this man was trying to go somewhere that he wasn't supposed to go and the donkey kept trying to go the other way, but the man kept trying to make him go where he wanted him to go. Then the donkey started talking and told him that if they went that way something bad was going to happen to them! Mom, can animals talk for real?" he said, expressing what I thought was doubt in the lesson.

"If God allows them to," I answered, taking him by his hand.

"God can use anything to talk to people?" He peered up at me with his bright eyes.

"Yes, baby."

"Even a little kid?"

"Even a little kid," I confirmed. CJ was silent for the next several seconds as we walked to the car, Jaxon greeting his brothers and sisters in Christ along the way.

"Brother McAllister, how you doing, man?" a tall

man greeted with a handshake, then peeled out of his choir robe and draped it across his arm.

"Wonderful, man, wonderful. God is doing great things in my life." He flashed a smile and nodded deliberately as he bit into his bottom lip. "This is Jream Colton," he introduced, "and her children, Caryn and CJ. This is Patrick Underwood," he said back to us.

"Pleased to meet you, Sis," Patrick said kindly, with a single nod, glancing at the three of us.

"Listen, I wanted to check with you to see if you would still be able to help out next week with setting up the scaffold and getting those blown bulbs changed in the sanctuary." While Jaxon discussed those details, CJ tugged at my hand.

"Mom?" he started.

"Yes, baby."

"God told me to tell you that you've had your time to be hurt and to stop running from Him."

This time Jaxon did pretty much have to carry me out.

# Chapter 10

The doorbell rang, stirring me from my sleep. All I wanted today was to be left alone. The kids were spending Christmas in Arizona with Cade's sister and her family, and I'd let everyone I knew know that all I wanted for Christmas was to sleep late and have some private rest and rejuvenation time. So who was it that decided not to honor my request? The bell chimed a second time, ignoring the fact that I'd pulled the covers tightly over my head. The third ringing caused me to sling the covers back in anger and stomp over to the window. Peeking through the blinds, I didn't see a car that I recognized, only kids skateboarding, roller-skating, bike riding or tossing balls back and forth amongst themselves. "Who is it!" I mumbled as I pulled away from the window, crunched my brows downward and yanked my robe from the hook on the outside of my closet door, then stomped my way downstairs. Tying the belt firmly around my waist to cover my panties and bra, I peered through the peephole to see Jaxon holding a large box, just beginning to turn away to leave.

I really didn't feel like company, especially male company, since I hadn't even washed my face or brushed my teeth or hair. Even so, I felt bad about letting Jaxon just walk away, so I found myself pulling the door open.

Hearing the sound of the door crack, he jerked his head toward me and a smile spread across his face as he took quick steps toward the door. I pushed the storm door open, shuddering from the cold as I let him inside.

"Merry Christmas."

"Merry Christmas to you. It's barely eight o'clock in the morning," I answered more dryly than I really intended. I ran a hand over my hair, which I was sure was all over my head, then covered my mouth, remembering my untamed morning breath.

"Are you gonna be a Scrooge all day today?"

"I'll be right back." A single hand waved him toward the couch while I climbed the steps on my way to making myself a little more presentable. "Make yourself at home."

I had mixed feelings about Jaxon coming over. It felt good to know that he thought enough of me to come over bearing gifts on Christmas Day. On the other hand, I didn't want to get too involved. I felt a little guilty because I had only gotten him a couple of things for Christmas—assuming that the big box he carried was for me.

The longer I stood at the sink, running water as I brushed my teeth, the more I longed for the comfort of a relaxing shower. I thought about it for a few seconds, reasoning that Jaxon would be just fine for a few minutes, then started the shower, promising myself that I wouldn't take my usual twenty minutes.

By the time I made it back downstairs, refreshed, scented in Victoria's Secret Rapture, dressed in a red velour jogging suit, comfy fuzzy socks and fresh breath, with my hair pulled back in a ponytail, I could smell the aroma of pancakes and bacon wafting from my kitchen. Donny Hathaway's "This Christmas" played through the speakers of the intercom system, setting a cozy, seasonal mood. My lips pressed together in a slight twist, fighting back the urge to grin. "You really did make yourself at home, huh?"

"That's what you told me to do, right?" he asked rhetorically. "Nothing like a delicious breakfast on Christmas morning." Jaxon placed a steaming cup of hot chocolate, complete with whipped cream, on the table beside my prepared plate. He walked over and planted a light kiss on my cheek. "Merry Christmas," he said again, taking my hand and guiding me to take a seat.

"Thank you."

"My pleasure." He took a seat across from me, then gathered my hands into his own, preparing to say grace. While he closed his eyes, I rolled mine toward the ceiling, only half listening to his words of thanks. *Yadda yadda yadda,* I thought, but commented "amen" appropriately when he ended the short prayer.

"So, did you get everything you wanted?" I asked, chewing on a mouthful of the fluffiest and most buttery pancakes I'd ever tasted in my life. "Mmm!"

"My grandma's secret recipe." He bobbed his head

proudly, enjoying watching me take pleasure in devouring his cooking. "I think I did get everything I wanted. I'm living another day, I'm healthy and strong, and I'm here having breakfast with you." He shrugged quickly. "What else could I possibly want?"

"A million dollars."

"I'm rich in the spirit," he readily replied.

*Whatever,* I thought, although I nodded. *Stop being so deep.*

"How about you? Did Santa bring you everything on your list?" He broke off a crisp piece of bacon and nibbled on it.

"I didn't really have a list. That way there'd be no disappointment if I didn't get what I would have asked for."

"Well, I did bring you a little something."

"Did you really? You know you didn't have to do that."

"I did it because it makes my heart happy to see you smile." I couldn't help but blush. "How's your breakfast?"

"It's great." I nodded. "Who needs IHOP and Denny's when the world has you?" Jaxon chuckled. We finished our meals without words while "The Christmas Song" resonated through the house. Jaxon impressed me further when he stood and cleared the table, rinsed the dishes and placed them in the dishwasher. I sat at the table with my chin resting in my palms, just watching him.

"Come on in here so you can open your gift." He led the way to my living room, as if he lived there, lifted the box he'd brought in from under the tree and handed it to me.

"What is it?" I asked, shaking the box slightly.

"Do you want me to tell you or would you rather open it and see?" he countered, with raised brows.

Jaxon couldn't contain his smile as I unwrapped the large box meticulously covered in green-and-gold paper. It was filled with other small packages, all neatly wrapped in varied paper. Taped to the inside lid was a CD marked *Play me first* in beautiful calligraphic writing. Without a word, I rose to my feet and padded over to the CD player to follow the instructions. A jazzy rendition of "My Favorite Things" began to play as I stuck my hand inside the box and pulled out the first wrapped gift. I quickly pulled the paper off, to find a small box holding a diamond cross pendant necklace.

"I know how much a woman likes diamonds," he said when I gasped in complete surprise. He took the box from my hands, freed the necklace and stood behind me to clasp it around my neck.

"Thank you, Jaxon," I said, feeling around my neckline, with a wide grin on my face.

"You're welcome." The next box I opened held a sterling silver pen-and-pencil set engraved with my name. "Since you sign paychecks every week, I thought you should do it in style. A regular Paper Mate pen just doesn't suit you."

Excitedly I jumped up, ran into my office and came back with a legal pad. With a smile, I signed my name several times over, enjoying the way the pen rolled smoothly across the paper. "This is nice. Thank you again."

"It's only what you deserve. There's more." He motioned back toward the box.

Next I pulled out a journal, a set of two ceramic heart-shaped keepsake boxes, a set of four Brazilian agate bowls and, last but not least, a long velvet box holding a stunning seven-inch emerald tennis bracelet. I hadn't had a Christmas like this since I was eleven years old and got nearly everything I'd put on my list, including a Cabbage Patch doll, Barbie's Dream House, with the matching pink convertible, and an Easy-Bake Oven, with four extra boxes of cake mix. I felt like a kid all over again.

"Jaxon, I don't have nearly as much stuff for you as you have for me."

"Babe, I didn't get you these things expecting the same in return. I got you these because I wanted you to have them. I wanted to see you smile." And that I did . . . again.

"Let me get your gifts." I had selected two sets of neckties, handkerchiefs and cufflinks, and a leather watch case bearing his monogram. He opened them gleefully and thanked me with a kiss on the cheek.

Glancing down at his watch, he suddenly jumped to his feet and grabbed me by the wrist. "Come on, I have a surprise for you. Get your coat."

"What is it, Jaxon?"

"It's a surprise, babe. Do you want me to tell you or do you want to be surprised? Get your coat, hat and gloves, and come on," he instructed. It took me a second too long to move, prompting him to say, "Come on, Jream!"

"All right, all right!" I shrieked with a smirk, excited about what he had in store. I tried to guess where we were headed once we got in the car, but I would have never guessed a day trip to New York City.

Within two hours, we'd made it through both Newport News/Williamsburg International and LaGuardia Airports, hopped into a cab and were headed for Rockefeller Center. At this point, I was totally blown away, and grinning like Cesar Romero dressed as the Joker from *Batman*. Jaxon held my hand during the cab ride, intermittently looking at me to interpret my expression. He couldn't have seen anything else other than happiness. Like a child, I oohed and aahed at the holiday busyness, and I really felt like I was in a movie once we pulled up in front of the plaza and I saw with my very own eyes the huge lit Christmas tree.

Jaxon paid the driver and together we stepped into the bitter cold. It felt like a hundred degrees below zero to me, but my fly-away date was warming enough, although I wished I had on some thicker pants. As if Jaxon could read my mind, he tugged at my arm.

"You wanna run in here and get some extra sweats," he asked, pointing to a nearby store.

"Yeah, that would be great." I shuddered as we jetted, hand in hand, across the street.

While we browsed around the store, I took note of the time, which was shortly after noon, so I reasoned that the kids would be up by now. Especially CJ. I pulled out my cell and dialed my sister-in-law's number.

"Merry Christmas," she answered after a few rings. In the background, I could hear all kinds of whizzing, ringing and electronic noises, along with laughter, paper being torn off boxes and gasps.

"You all up and at 'em already, huh?" I smiled.

"Oh, hey, girl," Dawn answered jovially. "Yeah, we're in here having a good old time. Thanks for letting the kids come out." Dawn and her husband, Franklin, had four kids of their own, two teenage daughters, Angie and Sabrina, and two six-year-old twin boys, Marcus and Michael, so both Caryn and CJ were in good company.

"You're welcome. I think they needed a little change in scenery. It's been a rough year." There was a bit of a pause while we both remembered Cade. "So how are they doing?" I started again.

"Caryn and the girls have reunited and made up for every single day they've not seen each other, and, girl, I don't even have to tell you about these rambunctious boys! You don't hear them in here tearing up my family room?" She chuckled.

"Better your place than mine." I laughed with her. "Well, let me speak to them for a few minutes."

"Sure, hold on a sec," Dawn said before pulling the phone away from her face to prevent screaming in my ear. "CJ, sweetie, your mom's on the phone!" she yelled over the noise of Christmas Day excitement.

"Yay!" I heard him shriek. In seconds his overly stimulated voice hit my eardrums. "Hi, Mom, Merry Christmas! Ho, ho, ho!" he puffed out in his best impression of Santa Claus.

"Hey, baby boy! Merry Christmas to you! So what all did you get?" CJ began naming the items that I'd shipped to Dawn and Frank's a week ago.

"You were right, Mom! Santa did know that I was

going to be at Aunt Dawn's house, and he brought me everything!"

"See, I told you," I replied, beaming just from the joy in his voice.

"We should come back every year so we can have two Christmases again!" he suggested, pleasantly overwhelmed by having a Christmas celebration at home before he and Caryn left two days ago, and then having another this morning.

"I don't know about that CJ, but we'll see."

"Okay!" he said as excitedly as if I'd agreed to his proposal.

"Let me speak to your sister."

"All right, bye—love you!"

"Love you too, babe." At that, he dropped the phone and went screaming through the house, calling for Caryn.

"I got it!" There were a few seconds of clattering as the phone was being hung up in another room; then suddenly the sound of a thousand toys dropped from the background, replaced by a Chris Brown song. "Hello?"

"Hey, sweetie, Merry Christmas."

"Merry Christmas to you, Mom."

"Are you enjoying yourself?"

"Yes!" I could tell she was smiling, and it did my heart good to know that she was in better spirits. "Thanks for letting us come."

"You're welcome. Did you get your things?" Caryn's gifts consisted mostly of gift cards to her favorite stores, then a few other clothing and grooming items I'd picked out and sent.

"Yes, I love those H&M jeans, and Angie and

Sabrina and me are going shopping tomorrow as soon as the mall opens."

"Sounds good."

"So what about you? What are you doing today?"

"Ummm . . . I'm in New York right now."

"New York? Mom, you went to New York without me?"

"I didn't mean to. Jaxon showed up this morning with a couple of tickets and whisked me away," I said, winking my eye at him as he took our selection of sweats, extra hats, and thicker gloves to the counter.

"Bring me something, Mom."

"Of course, I will."

"A purse," she threw in. "Prada."

"We'll see. Anyway, let me go. I just wanted to wish you a Merry Christmas and let you know that I love you."

"Love you too."

"Enjoy the rest of your trip and I'll see you in a couple of days."

"Okay, Mom. Bye."

I sighed with a smile as I closed my phone and slid it back into my pocket, then snuggled up against Jaxon's arm. I'm not quite sure what made me do that. I guess it was just the Christmas spirit and hearing happiness in my children's voices— especially Caryn's.

Jaxon paid for our things; then the clerk allowed me to use a dressing room to put my extra garments on. It took me a few minutes to pad up a bit; then I did something I'd never done before, which was put on a pair of ice skates. Jaxon had his on in minutes, mentioned that he'd be right back, then took to the ice like an Olympic medalist. He did some double-triple-toe-axel stuff and some swirly fast-spinning-with-his-leg-out stuff and some wide-legged-stance leaning-forward stuff. I swear he did everything besides jump up and touch his toes. And with every little trick, I clapped and cheered. Finally he coasted toward me.

"Okay, I'm all warmed up now," he huffed. "You ready?"

"Yep! It's time for me to show you what I can do." When I tried to stand up, I felt like a newborn colt just getting used to its legs. I shook, wobbled, grasped at the air and held on to Jaxon's arm for dear life while he laughed like Santa Claus. Patiently Jaxon took me around the rink, saving me from numerous falls when others whizzed by me as fast as cars on the highway. After a few loops around, I finally got the hang of it a little bit, and was able to slowly coast with Jaxon, holding hands like teenagers and giggling at my success.

When we'd had enough, we eased off the ice, got back into our shoes and walked to Starbucks to grab a hot beverage and knock the chill off a bit.

"That was so much fun," I said, practically skipping as I swung his hand with mine.

"I'm glad you enjoyed it." He tugged on my scarf with a smile.

"So how'd you learn to skate like that?"

"My mom made my sister and me take lessons when we were little." He shrugged. "I guess I just kinda stuck with it in my spare time, since it used to impress people when I was a teen. I thought about playing ice hockey a few times, but I value my teeth too much."

"I can understand that," I said, beginning to shiver just as we reached Starbucks doorway. I ordered a Grande Cinnamon Dolce Latte and Jaxon ordered a cup of plain black coffee; then we took a seat in front of a window. We sipped from our cups, gazing into each other's eyes until we both started to blush—me feeling like a high-school girl on a first date. I didn't even remember feeling like that with Cade.

"Are you enjoying yourself?" he asked, blowing into his cup.

"Today has been amazing," I answered. "I'd planned on just staying in bed and letting the day pass uneventfully, but I'm glad you had something else in mind."

"I couldn't let you spend Christmas Day alone. What fun is that?"

"I wasn't looking to have any fun, I guess." I shrugged. "I was just trying to make it through to tomorrow. Just taking things one day, one hour, one minute, at a time."

Jaxon folded his lips into his mouth in pensive thought. "Don't you want more out of life than that, though?" he asked, studying my eyes. "I mean, what joy is there in struggling just to make it until the next minute? You have so much more to live for than another hour of the day."

"Like what," I asked, feeling a gradual moroseness settle over me. I couldn't keep my eyes focused on him anymore, so I looked out the window at the scores of people bustling by.

"Well, for one, your children. Aren't they worth living for? Aren't they something to look forward to?"

"Of course, they are," I answered right away, more out of instinct than out of thought. Although had I reflected on it, my answer would have been the same.

"And look at what you've done with your store. That place is incredible! I remember what it looked like before and there is just no comparing the two. Look at all that you've been able to do with it. It's like one of the city's hot spots for women now. You gotta love that," he encouraged.

"That came at the expense of a broken heart, though. If I had to choose between losing my husband and revamping Sweet Jream's, I would have picked Cade on any day."

"But that choice was not yours to make, Jream. You didn't choose for your husband to die, did you?" I didn't respond. "You had a barrel of lemons, you made lemonade, and all I am saying to you is drink some. Enjoy some. Because you know what will happen if you don't?"

"What?" I muttered.

"Either someone's gonna drink it for you, then you'll really be mad, or it will sit there and spoil and go to waste," he said in a matter-of-fact tone. "And, babe, what you are doing is letting your lemonade go to waste."

I brooded over his words while we finished our coffees in silence. He was right. My lemonade was spoiling.

"You ready?" he asked softly. I nodded. "We have

some more time before we have to head back to the
airport, so let's go," he finished, grabbing my hand.


We bundled up, stepped out into the cold and
jetted toward an empty taxi. "Seventeen West 125th,"
Jaxon instructed as we climbed into the backseat. The
driver acknowledged with a bob of his head, jerked
into traffic and weaved, bobbed, swerved, sped forward, slammed on brakes, cursed, complained and
murmured all the way into Harlem. As if he didn't
see it coming, he suddenly swerved a final time in
front of a Caribbean and soul food restaurant.

Upon my entrance, sand-colored walls and rich-
toned décor, along with jazzy music, immediately
soothed my spirits. The ambiance was perfect.
Though crowded, we were soon seated at a small
table against the wall, since Jaxon had made reser-
vations. He helped me out of my coat, pecked my
cheek, then sat down and smiled at me. I couldn't
help but smile back.

"Thanks for bringing me here."

"Thanks for coming," he said right before we
were greeted by our server. She took our drink order
and left us with menus to browse. Everything
looked and sounded so scrumptious, I had a hard
time selecting a meal. Since I wanted to taste so
many things, we decided to order an appetizer of
deep-fried whiting strips with curry pineapple
sauce; then for an entrée, I selected the hot and
spicy chicken marinated in a homemade jerk sauce
infused with pimento, grilled on a cedar plank, with
a side of rice and peas. Jaxon chose the pan-fried

chicken smothered in a rich brown gravy of onions, tomatoes and bell peppers, with the agreement that we would share everything that hit the table.

Ironically, I thought of Cade. He hated to share his food with me, oftentimes stating that I should have ordered what I wanted to eat.

Between feeding himself, Jaxon fed me forkful after forkful of the dishes on the table, no matter whose plate it was on. The food was so delicious, somebody's momma needed to be slapped. Had I not been in New York, I may have tried it!

"How do you do it, Jaxon?" I asked as we finished off our entrées.

"How do I do what? Stay so fine?" he teased. I couldn't help but giggle.

"Well, that too, but how do you stay so . . . on top of the world?" I described with a shrug and tossed-up hands. "So optimistic, so . . . at peace with the world, like nothing ever goes wrong in your life?"

Jaxon guffawed. "Well, that's hardly true. I've had so many disappointments and setbacks in my life, that at one point I just didn't want to live another day." He shook his head slowly as he focused on an invisible spot on the wall adjacent to our table. "I didn't tell you this, but my mother died right in my arms," he said somberly as he looked directly in my eyes and folded his lips inward. "Bled to death . . . after my dad stabbed her fourteen times and left her for dead." I gasped, but otherwise kept silent as I reasoned that that was why his father was serving time. "Jamillah was away at college and no one else was at the house but me. I came in the house after a basketball game, and there she was, lying on the

144     *Kimberly T. Matthews*

living-room floor, gasping for air." Tears burned in my eyes just imagining such a horrific scene. "And I held on to her until I couldn't anymore." He pressed a closed fist to his lips and blew inside as if he were trying to warm his hands. "I've never felt anything that hurt so bad," he said just above a whisper. "And I just kept waiting for my heart to explode right inside my chest . . . but when it didn't, I found out that I had to keep on living. And it was hard"—he nodded— "really hard. My mom was gone, I didn't know what to think of my dad. I loved him—I hated him. . . ." His voice trailed off as he seemed to get lost in his thoughts. Suddenly he seemed to snap out of it.

"So how would you feel if you gave me a gift, something you spent time shopping for and spent your money on, or made it or whatever, and I took it, barely looked at it, and then just threw it in the trash?" In demonstration he crumpled up a napkin and tossed it over his shoulder onto the floor. "And I just didn't do it one time, but I did it every single time you gave me something." Several more napkins flew over his shoulder in rapid succession.

"Okay, Jaxon," I said, grabbing at his hand to stop him. "You're wasting the people's stuff and making a mess."

"You see what you are doing—you're stopping me. You don't want me to waste any more napkins. You didn't even give me these. You didn't pay for them. You don't care about them, but you don't want me to waste them or make a mess. Right?"

"Mmm . . . I guess."

"Well, one day I realized that that is what I was doing. Wasting my life and making a mess—balling up every single day and tossing it in the trash. I finally came to the realization that every day that God allowed me to wake up—living, breathing and in my right mind—was a gift to me. You ever heard that before?"

"What?" I questioned softly.

"Every day is a gift—that's why it is called the present."

"I think so."

"Well, it is, and I've learned to treat it as such. Come hell or high water."

I nodded, with a smile. "Good philosophy."

We topped the meal with the restaurant's highly appraised Rummy Rum cake, which featured layers of delicious cake soaked in a blend of three vintage rums, and topped with vanilla ice cream. When I took the first bite, I started looking around for Moses, Jacob, Noah and a couple of angels, because it was pure heaven. By the time we left, the cake had given me such a buzz that I thought I really saw them on the way out. It was a good thing neither of us was driving.

Another cab whisked us back to the airport, where we quickly boarded our flight and headed back to Virginia. I slept against Jaxon's arm all the way home, then dozed off again, once we got in his car. On my doorstep, he graciously took my keys, although I wasn't drunk . . . I don't think, let me in my home, then kissed me good night.

"Good night to you too, Jaxon," I said, hugging

him as tightly as I could. "And thanks for the best Christmas ever."

I climbed in my bed with a smile reflecting on the details of my wonderful day. Before I could close my eyes in sweet repose, the phone by my bed rang.

"Hello," I sang jovially.

"Jream, it's Dawn. Sorry to be calling you so late."

"It's all right. What's wrong. Are the kids okay?"

"Yeah, they're all right. I'm just terribly disturbed about something and thought I should bring it to your attention."

"Okay." I sighed inaudibly.

"Well, the girls had some company over this evening to play games and stuff, and, apparently, one of the games Caryn ended up playing with a couple of the neighbor boys was spin the bottle, if you know what I mean."

"Oh, my goodness. Dawn, I am so sorry. So . . . I mean, what she'd . . . how'd she . . ." I was trying to ask for the gory details without actually asking, and Dawn didn't force me.

"I happened to go down in the basement to get a couple of bottles of wine for the adults, and lo and behold, there it was right out in front of me." I could do nothing but sigh again, but this time heavily. "I did talk to her about it a little bit, and her excuse was that you knew she was having sex and had her put on the pill."

My mouth flew open as I stuttered to find words. "Well, I—I mean I did . . . see I found out that—" I stopped and took a deep breath as my eyes filled with tears. Then I slowly started again. "I've been having such a rough time with her, Dawn."

Dawn listened for the next hour or so, while I openly shared with her Caryn's behaviors and how disappointed I was. She listened, only commenting "mmm-hmm" when necessary for acknowledgment.

"I'm just so sorry she'd brought that foolishness to your house," I ended. "Do you need to send her home early?"

"No, I don't want to do that, but I'm going to have some pretty strict boundaries around her while she's here. I was going to let Angie drive them out to the mall tomorrow, but I guess I will have to chaperone that little excursion myself."

Again I apologized for my daughter's behavior, then thanked Dawn for calling.

It wasn't such a great Christmas after all.

# Chapter 11

The merchandise tables had been cleared away and both of the store's sofas had been brought together, making an expanded living-room setting. A table holding champagne-filled glasses, smoked barbeque ribs, mini chicken quesadillas, mozzarella sticks and battered mushrooms sat along the wall, just below a collage of photos of the happy couple. Just as the final touches were put into place, Alonzo pulled up in his Land Rover. He let Tweet out of the passenger side as we hovered in a corner, peering through the tinted window. She tapped on the door, cupping her hand around her eyes to see against the glare of the streetlight behind her, and saw me moving toward the door with a smile. I twisted the lock and let her and Alonzo inside, and at the same time, Shanice flipped the light switch on.

"Surprise!" a host of people yelled at Tweet. Her fiancé, Alonzo Percy, and I had worked together to pull off a surprise engagement party. I had convinced her that I was holding a mandatory staff meeting after the store closed, which wasn't hard to pull off, since I always scheduled staff meetings for Sunday evenings, and she hadn't been the wiser. The expression on her face had been priceless as she was greeted by her friends and loved ones, offering congratulations and hugs.

I moved off to the side, watching her gloat, and backed into Jaxon's arms, which he casually wrapped around my shoulders. The span of his chest felt so good against my back. He pressed a kiss into my neck and squeezed me a little, which made me smile.

"You did a great job setting this up, Jream," he commented over my shoulder.

"Thanks." I tilted my head back and pecked his smooth lips. "You want something to eat?"

"Yeah, but let me serve you. You've done enough work for the day." He gently released me, greeted Alonzo with a handshake and Tweet with a brief hug, then visited the food table, laughing and smiling with the other guests. I didn't mean to stare, but I couldn't take my eyes off him.

"Jream, where did you put the cake server?" Michetta asked. "And stop ogling that man so hard," she teased. "We know he's fine and you can't help it, but try, okay?"

"Was I drooling?"

"Yes, girl. You almost need a bib." We chuckled together while I went to the back and returned with the requested utensil, then returned back to where Jaxon was waiting for me with a filled plate.

Tweet was in the middle of explaining to her guest how she and Alonzo had met. "So I was standing there, just looking a hot mess—a scarf on my head, clothes wrinkled, a wife beater and a pair of run-down flip-flops, with chipped toe nail polish—just running in the store to get some milk for my coffee."

"But I saw past all of that and saw a queen," Alonzo interjected, pulling Tweet to him by her waist.

"Anyway, when he happened to come here a few days later, we started talking and the rest is history."

"Yeah, but who was he in here trying to shop for?" Tweet's mom, Mrs. Johnson, asked, causing an eruption of laughter and comments.

"See, that's grown folks' business right there." Alonzo chuckled. At that point, the playful roasting and speeches started, with both their families taking turns sharing funny stories.

In perfect hostess fashion, Michetta had begun facilitating an icebreaker game. She'd split the group into guys versus girls and stood in the middle of the floor with a stack of index cards. "All right, let's start with the bride-to-be!" she screamed, grabbing Tweet by the hand and pulling her up from the sofa. "Okay, sing a song that has the word 'kiss' in it."

"'Every time you kiss me . . .'" Tweet began fumbling and stumbling through Alicia Keys's "Like You'll Never See Me Again," singing and tearing through the lyrics in a way that would have probably made Alicia want to sue, but was making us all chuckle.

"Okay, your turn, Alonzo." Michetta coaxed him to standing. "Same thing—sing a song with the word 'kiss' in it."

Without hesitation Alonzo flashed a pair of devilish bedroom eyes and licked the palm of his hand as he changed his voice to a crazy falsetto. "'You don't have to be rich to be my girl, you don't have to be cool to rule my world . . .'" We all burst into laughter and applause, singing the next two lines with him, complete with the smooching sound, while Alonzo spun in circles and attempted a split, but didn't quite make it.

"'Kiss'!" we all yelled on cue, falling over each other at Alonzo's hilarious act. There was no question that the men took the point. Once we composed ourselves, Michetta moved on to the second question, calling on me and Jaxon.

"Come on up here, Jream." I acted reluctant and shy as I trudged forward, but, secretly, I was ready to score a point for the girls.

"Okay. Sing a song with the word 'love.'" Right away the men gathered in a circle and began collaborating on what they wanted Jaxon to sing. When the ladies saw this, they did the same, shrieking for me to consult with them first. A few seconds later, I was ready to perform. With a borrowed hairbrush in my hand, I fluffed up the braids that I'd just happened to have curled that day and opened my mouth to let out my most sultry voice.

"'Uhhhh, love to love you, baby . . . uhhhhh, love to love you baby.'" I slowly lowered myself from standing to crouching, then back to standing again, as I sang a little Donna Summer, then sauntered to my seat, gaining the cheers of my team.

Jaxon stood, hitching up his pants, and took the stage. With a smile and snapping fingers, he began singing through his nose.

"'I'm so in love with you, awww, whatever you

wanna do, is all right with meeeeee!'" He screeched, reaching for a high note. "'Le-eh-eh-et's, let's stay togethaaaa.'" His boys backed him with vocals for his rendition of the Al Green classic, while we ladies laughed and clapped for them, then joined in on "'times are good or bad, happy or sad.'"

Our singing was abruptly interrupted by loud banging on the door that scared us all and commanded our immediate attention. We could only make out the silhouette of a large man, who was not shy about his intent to get in the shop, signified by more banging. Jaxon audaciously, but cautiously, approached the door. He didn't open it right away, while every other man stood to his feet, ready to defend and protect the women there.

"Can I help you?" Jaxon asked.

"Where Michetta at?" he demanded, muffled by the glass.

Jaxon turned toward us and looked at Michetta. "You know him," he asked, nodding toward the door.

"Oh Lord." She rolled her eyes, then dropped her head in embarrassment as she walked toward the door. Jaxon stood back slightly to let Michetta by. She twisted the lock and opened the door to step out. "What are you doing here, LaVeil?" She closed the door behind her and they both moved closer to the curb, and out of our hearing range—even if they were yelling, which it was clear, through their body language, that they were.

We watched for a few seconds as their arms flailed about, they pointed fingers at each other, crossed arms across their chests, turned their backs and shouted inaudible words back and forth. It was difficult to get back to the party and not be instinctively drawn to their distraction, although we did try. Before we could, however, Michetta and LaVeil's argument turned physical as we watched him grab her by her hair and slam her against a nearby car.

"Call the police," Shanice ordered, "he's hitting her!" Several people dug through their purses for cell phones, while a couple of the guys ran outside to rescue Michetta, including Jaxon.

"Ay, man! Ay! Calm down," he shouted as he stepped onto the pavement. It didn't take much for the three men to pull LaVeil away from Michetta, allowing her to dash into the store in tears, while LaVeil shouted obscenities behind her.

"Something going on up in there, all these men sitting around, and you want me to believe you ain't breakin' none of 'em off!? You must think I'm crazy!"

"I'm sorry, Tweet," she mumbled, rushing toward the back room, humiliated.

The men stayed outside with LaVeil until two officers slowly approached and took charge of a now-diffused situation. After a few minutes, one tapped on the door and was met by me.

"Good evening, ma'am. Is the young lady still here?" he asked.

"Yes, she's in the back, come on in." I escorted him to the back room, motioning for Shanice to join him for Michetta's support. She leapt to her feet and followed the officer through the back doorway, while I tried to manage the guests and keep an eye on what was going on outside. It wasn't much longer before LaVeil got in his car and eased away, freeing the men to come back inside, along with the second cop.

I pointed the way to the back room, then met back with Jaxon, with inquisitive eyes.

He only slightly nodded as he said, "Everything's all right," although we both knew that ultimately it wasn't.

Chatter was beginning to grow once more as we tried to get back into a celebratory mood. Tweet's mom took over as the game facilitator, doing her best to re-create the fun atmosphere that had been present twenty minutes before. While she started the guests on the next song, Jaxon and I hung more to the back, keeping a watchful eye on things. Shanice appeared in the back room's doorway and motioned for me.

"Be right back," I whispered to Jaxon before moving toward Shanice.

"I'm going to tiptoe out and take her home," Shanice shared. Michetta just stood dejectedly silent, waiting at the back door. "Can you let us out the back way? Michetta doesn't want to further distract the party," she whispered.

"Sure. Let me grab my keys." Once I updated Jaxon on what was going on, he escorted me to the back, then saw both ladies to their cars and returned to the party minutes later, which had gotten as much back to normal as it possibly could have.

The two teams were working on the word "forever," and the guys were headed for a score with Heatwave's "Always and Forever" as Tweet's dad serenaded her mom with a long stream of "'for-eh-eh-eh-eh-eh-eh-eh-eh-eh-eh . . .'" He lowered himself to bended knee, and in an instant, the howls, laughter and clapping were back.

Shortly after, the soon-to-be-wed couple sat together on the sofa and opened gifts, thanking everyone for the collection of dinner gift cards, movie passes, bottles of champagne and wines, and a pair of matching T-shirts that read *Taken.*"

"One day this will be us," Jaxon murmured. "And we'll sit on the couch, open gifts and smile."

"You think so?"

"I know it." He nodded. "I'm sure of it . . . if you let me in there," he added, tapping on my chest.

"You're already in there." I spoke with enough apprehension that I couldn't bring myself to look in his eyes while I said it. Instead, I pretended to be studying a piece of rib, the number of tines on my fork and how much Colby-Jack cheese had oozed from my quesadilla and onto my plate. I studied my food for a few seconds, and when I thought it was safe, I glanced up at Jaxon, only to find that he was staring at me. Quickly I shifted my eyes to the guests.

"You're afraid," he spoke softly. "You're afraid to move forward, Jream, because you're holding on to hurt."

"No. It's not that," I denied, although Jaxon was exactly right. I was afraid. Afraid to invest emotionally, afraid to let go of Cade's memory. Afraid to move forward with my life romantically. Afraid that the past would somehow repeat itself and break my heart all over again.

"Look at me, Jream," Jaxon gently commanded. I didn't do it right away, but I complied and met Jaxon with my eyes. "Listen to what I'm going to say to you." His eyes bounced back and forth between mine as he brought his face closer. "Sometimes extreme pain is what's necessary to bring forth another beautiful and amazing part of life. Look at the beauty of your children." He paused pensively to give me time to think on what he'd just said, then continued. "From what I've been told, bringing a child into this world is an extremely laborious and painful process. But you survived it . . . twice."

*What do you know about having babies?* I thought, becoming internally defensive.

"You are a beautiful, incredibly intriguing woman, and I love you, Jream." Did this man just tell me that he loved me? That statement soothed my little defensiveness right away. "We've all experienced not-so-pleasant events in our lives that maybe made us regret our very existence. We've all been hurt, babe. But you've got to know that a little hurt ain't never hurt nobody," he said, shaking his head slowly, then leaned in to kiss my lips as he clasped my hands into his own.

As much as I tried, I couldn't pull my eyes away from his. He held me captive with the love that radiated from his intent look.

"We're going to head on out," I heard one of the guests say. "Jream, you did a great job setting this up, and I will definitely be back to shop!" I looked away from Jaxon to see Tweet's sister, Dina, coming toward me for a quick hug.

"Thank you for coming," I said, smiling pleasantly. Dina's departure began a chain reaction of people gathering their things and trickling out the door, while my staff began collecting trash and cleaning up.

"Jream!" Tweet trotted over to me with extended

arms. "Thank you so much!" We embraced tightly and she rocked me from side to side. "You're the best boss ever."

"You're so welcome. It was my pleasure. I am so happy for you and Alonzo and wish you all the best in your lives together." I nodded sincerely. "And even if Alonzo turns you into a housewife and stay-at-home mom, I still expect you to keep him satisfied by buying all your lingerie and intimate garments from here!" I ordered.

"Oh, you don't have to worry about that! She's gonna be a lifelong customer. I think it was that outfit right there"—he pointed to a manikin that was scantily dressed in a black fishnet chemise— "that made me fall in love with her."

Tweet smacked Alonzo on the arm. "See! You done said too much, you done said too much!" she reprimanded, suddenly embarrassed. "They don't need to know what's in my closet."

"I'm the one that rang you up, Tweet," I reminded.

"Oh. Oh yeah." She giggled. "I do work here, don't I?"

"You two have a good night, and I'll see you in the morning." I laughed as Jaxon and I saw them both to the door.

It took thirty more minutes for the store to clear of all guests, and Shanice and Stephanie stayed another half hour, helping Jaxon and me reset the store. After dimming the lights, the four of us collapsed on the furniture, letting out exhaustive sighs.

"What a night," Shanice commented, nibbling on a piece of cake.

"Yeah," Stephanie added, "I hope Michetta is

okay, and it's too bad that that's the highlight of the evening."

"Only if you all allow it to be," Jaxon commented, rising to his feet and stretching. Taking his cue, no one spoke another word about the evening's unpleasant events.

"Well, let me get on outta here. I'll be here in the morning, Jream," Shanice said, standing, followed by Stephanie.

"Okay, ladies. Thanks for all your help tonight." Once I locked the doors, Jaxon pulled me into his arms and fully kissed me. His lips were warm and inviting, soft and smooth, supple and sexy. Before I knew it, a moan came forth from my vocal cords. The music system was still on, allowing Donell Jones to croon us into a slow dance, and little by little, my guard came down. The comfort and security I felt in Jaxon's arms brought a release of months of tension and frustration as I let myself become vulnerable.

I'm not quite sure how this happened, but somehow, someway, our footsteps eased us toward the corner of the exquisite bed display. With our lips gently joined, Jaxon delicately maneuvered me through the canopy's opening and guided me to lying down. His breathing was relaxed as our kisses grew more and more passionate. He tenderly stroked my hair and face, caressed my chin and looked at me with eyes filled with such adoration. There was no question about his sincerity in the words he'd spoken to me earlier. So I let go.

\* \* \*

Two hours later, nestled between the never-slept-on satin sheets, I lay against his chest, listening to him snore softly.

*"Is sex, sex, Jream?"* I heard God say. What did He mean by that? *"Is fornication, fornication?"* I was afraid to answer. *"Tell me how this is different from the behavior of your daughter."* My first thought was *I'm grown!* but He cut me off. *"Is sin, sin—regardless of age or situation?"*

I was stunned, ashamed and internally speechless. Lying still for another ten minutes, I tried to reason and justify how my sleeping with Jaxon in the middle of a retail store was *far* different from Caryn's shameful act. No matter what I thought of—my age, my perception of Jaxon's love for me, my maturity level, our responsibility in using condoms (which I kept in stock at the store), my ability to handle a sexual relationship—nothing substantiated my reasoning.

Now I felt incredibly guilty. Not so much because I'd had premarital sex with Jaxon, but because of the way I'd treated my daughter. I hadn't embraced her with loving kindness and gentle reproof, but instead I tore into her with such fury, that we'd barely spoken since. And it had been two months ago since I picked her up from school that day.

I slipped away from Jaxon, tiptoed around the store butt naked and pulled a couple of hygiene products and a pair of clean panties off the sales floor and ambled to the bathroom. Before waking Jaxon, I slipped into my clothes, went to the back room and pulled the extra display bedding down from a shelf. It was just past midnight when I shook him softly to arouse him from sleep. He stirred a bit, fluttered his eyes open and smiled at me, then pulled me toward him. I refrained from lying on his chest a second time, still consumed by guilt. Instead, I sat at his side and gazed into his eyes.

"What's wrong, babe?" I only shook my head. He rose up onto his elbows. "You sure?" This time I nodded. He studied my face for a minute, then sighed and spoke. "You were amazing." I blushed with embarrassment and looked away. Gently he touched my hand and continued. "You were amazing, but I owe you an apology. I love you and should have honored you by waiting." He momentarily stared up at the simulated stars in the ceiling, then floated his eyes back to mine. "I find you irresistible, but didn't honor you and the extraordinary woman that you are. Please forgive me," he whispered with remorse. I wasn't quite sure how to respond to that, other than by an almost undetectable nod of my head.

"Let's change these bedclothes and get out of here," I murmured. "I'll give you some privacy." I went in the back and leaned against the counter, my arms folded across my chest, thinking about what Jaxon had just said. "What kind of man sincerely apologizes after sex?" I mumbled aloud to myself.

*"For a just man falls seven times, and rises up again,"* God answered.

He sure was doing a lot of talking to me for us not to be on speaking terms.

# Chapter 12

"I filed," Michetta shared with me a couple of weeks later.

"What do you mean?"

"We're getting a divorce." I studied Michetta's expression, which was calm and composed. I knew that me asking if she was sure would be the wrong thing to say, so I said nothing. "I talked to my lawyer a couple of days ago and asked her to draw up the papers right away. The only thing is, they won't grant it until we have lived separate and apart for a whole year."

"Really?"

"Yeah. So I moved out and into a motel for now."

"In a motel?" I gasped.

"Girl, I gotta do what I gotta do. I've made up my mind that I'm calling it quits, and I'm not living there in that apartment with him, not another day," she said adamantly.

"But what about your stuff?"

"I don't care about that stuff. There ain't nothing at that house that can't be bought again, so as far as

I'm concerned, he can have it all. It's not worth my peace of mind and happiness."

"Well, where are you staying?"

"Suburban Lodge, on Hardy Cash Drive," she stated, referencing an extended-stay hotel. "It's just a little room with a kitchen sink, stove, toilet, a couple of dishes, a bed, TV and a small table-and-chair set. Girl, it's all I need right now. There is even a laundry facility in there, so I'm fine. I'm just glad we don't have any kids in the middle of all this."

"Isn't it expensive, though?"

"It ain't cheap, but I'm okay with it. Sometimes you just gotta sacrifice to get to where you need to be."

"Right," I agreed halfheartedly.

"So what about you and Jaxon? How is that going?"

I let out a smile-filled sigh and started snapping my fingers. "'I never knew love like this before. Now I'm lonely never more, since he came into my life'" I belted out the words to songstress Stephanie Mills's hit.

"Whaaaat!" she exclaimed. "Is it all that?"

"I'd never thought I'd say this, but I truly have never known a love like this . . . and you know Cade was a good husband."

"Yeah, I know—that's why I'm so surprised!"

"Jaxon is nothing but good to me. Real good," I admitted, partially thinking about the night we'd made love. I dared not share our little escapade, especially after the chastising I got behind it, but that didn't make it disappear from my mind. "Things are wonderful, and he is wonderful." I hadn't had the courage to say it before, but it was true.

"I kinda figured that from all those googly eyes you two were making at each other all night at the party."

"We were not," I gasped in denial.

"Oh yes, you were. You were looking just like this." She perched her hands beneath her chin and batted her lashes several times, then turned her head bashfully and faked a giggle.

"Whatever!" I laughed, slingshot-ing a pair of thongs over at her.

"And he was looking at you like he wanted to take you right over there," she said, pointing at the bed. "Hey! When did that get changed out?"

"That's been like that for a long time," I said, trying to avoid lying, and "long" was a relative term. I mean, a week is quick in comparison to a full year, but it's an extremely long time to have a toothache, right?

"I didn't remember seeing it like that at the party."

"That's because you were too busy playing hostess. You were focused on other things."

"Oh," she dismissed. "Anyway, I'm really happy for you, Jream. You seem happy and he seems like he is so good for you. How is he with the kids?"

"CJ *lovessssss* him," I exclaimed. "Now, Caryn, that little fast, hot-in-the-tail child doesn't say more than two words to anybody these days. Walking around the house with her lips glued together."

Michetta gave me a disapproving look. "Jream, I don't mean to get in your business, and you know I don't even have kids, but don't you think you need to be reaching out to her?"

"I am reaching out to her. She got somewhere to

lay her head at night, got food to put in her belly and clothes to wear on her back."

"Well, you owe her at least that, Jream. She is your child," she said. *Ouch!*

"Yeah, well, she owes me a few things too, like keeping her panties up and on," I defended.

"I'm just saying . . ." she shrugged. "The girl is hurting."

"She needs to be hurt. She'll be all right."

"But, Jream, you don't want her to continue to make bad decisions regarding men and end up destroyed."

"Long as she does what I tell her, she'll be just fine." Not wanting to hear another word, I changed the subject. "We need to send those baby dolls back to the vendor. They have the sizing all screwed up. Look at this mess." I walked over to a T-stand and yanked one of the garments from the hanger. "I can't get my right leg in this thing, and this is an extra large."

"I'll take care of it," Michetta responded, taking my subtle hint. We hardly said anything else to each other for the duration of my short workday.


Jaxon pulled a bouquet of fresh flowers from behind his back when I opened my front door. "Ta-da!" he sang. "Something for the dinner table."

"Thank you, Jaxon." I stood on my tiptoes to reach his lips for a peck. "Come on in, dinner is almost ready. How's your day been?"

"Typical, but it has significantly improved in the last"—he looked at the watch on his wrist—"ten seconds or so." Before handing me the flowers, he grabbed me in a tight bear hug. "Mmm! My dream come true. I missed you today," he whispered in my ear. "You know why?"

"Yes, because you knew I was cooking dinner and you got hungry while you were on that truck today."

"Well, that too, but that's not my number one reason." He circled his hands around my waist from behind and clumsily walked me into the kitchen while he nuzzled into my neck, causing me to giggle.

"Then why?" I stood at the stove, tossing the ingredients of pork stir-fry into my wok, then peeked into a small pot filled with rice.

"Because you're the best part of my day."

That had to be the sweetest thing I'd ever heard. I couldn't even find the words to respond to him, so I just leaned back against his chest, tilted my head upward and kissed him. "What am I going to do with you?" I questioned, smiling.

"If I told you, you wouldn't even believe me." He was probably going to say something like I was going to marry him eventually. Jaxon had already whispered in my ear many times that I was "the one," and as nice as it was to hear, I wasn't sure that I wanted to be his "the one," so I just blew off his comment with a forced chuckle.

"Do you want sweet tea or soda?" I asked, trying to shift gears.

"Whatever you fix me is fine." Jaxon released my waist and stepped back. "I'm going to go wash my hands. Where are the kids?"

"You know Caryn doesn't come downstairs unless I make her, and since you bought CJ that Wii thing, once he finishes his homework, I don't see the child anymore." I began transferring the food from the pots and pans on the stove into serving dishes. "He's probably grown a beard by now, I've not seen him in so long. Do you mind calling them down?"

"Not at all." Jaxon disappeared into the washroom in the hallway, freshened up a bit, then returned minutes later with both kids behind him.

"What did you do, send some telepathic message? I didn't even hear you call them."

"You just weren't listening, babe."

"What'd you cook? Something smells delicious!" CJ commented, rubbing his belly and taking a seat at the table.

"You'll see." I glanced at Caryn, waiting for her to say "Hi, Mom," "good evening, cat or dog," "kiss my foot" . . . something! This was my first time laying eyes on her today since she'd come in from school. Since the time she'd gotten suspended, she'd usually come in from working at the store, then go straight to her room without speaking a single word to anyone. She would stay there until the next morning. Tonight she had the evening off so that we could have dinner together as a family. My raised eyebrows and hard glare in her direction demanded that she speak.

"Hi, Mom. Good evening, Jaxon," she said sullenly.

"That's better." I turned my back and rolled my eyes when I was sure she couldn't see me. Trifling self. I didn't remember acting like that when I was sixteen. Like many adults my age, I had a mother who held a master's degree in knocking kids into next week, with an emphasis of slapping the black off a face. I had to wonder whose harvest I was reaping in Caryn's nasty attitude, because I definitely had not sown those seeds.

"So how was school?" Jaxon asked, like he did every time he saw the kids.

Caryn didn't even attempt to respond, but CJ burst into conversation like he'd been waiting all day to be asked that very question. "Awesome!" He began rambling about what he'd learned that day, explaining to Jaxon varied animal habitats. Jaxon humored him, acting as if he were hanging on every word, commenting "really?" "wow!" and "get out of here!" several times over, until I signaled that we needed to say grace.

Like always, we held hands around the table. I wouldn't have told anyone, but I was glad Caryn sat opposite me so that I didn't have to hold her hand. I mean, I loved my daughter, but I was still extremely disgusted, angry and frustrated with her.

Jaxon led the prayer, we all said amen in unison, then dug in.

"This is good, Jream," Jaxon complimented through a mouthful of food.

"Jaxon, you remind me of my daddy." I nearly choked on CJ's comment. Jaxon looked a bit taken aback himself. He swallowed and cleared his throat before speaking.

"Is that right?"

"Yep! 'Cause he used to always tell my mom that her food tasted good." CJ paused pensively, as if he were measuring his next words. "Are you going to be my next daddy?" I quickly jammed an egg roll in my mouth and shot my eyes at Jaxon. With complete ease, he answered.

"CJ, I could never be your daddy. Your daddy is someone that cannot be replaced. He will always be special to you and your sister and deserves to stay in your heart."

"Well, maybe not my daddy, but kinda like my daddy? Like, if you adopt me or something?"

"That's something that your mom gets to decide." I could have stuck Jaxon in his thigh with my fork for shifting all the weight on me like that. He looked at me with a smirk and twinkling eyes. I don't think my return glance was so pleasant.

"Mom, can Jaxon adopt me and Caryn?"

*"Pshhhhh!"* Caryn blew. I would have reprimanded her, but I wasn't ready to let on that I liked Jaxon as much as I did. I was afraid to love again. But still, she could have covered up her thoughts a little bit.

"We'll see, CJ. Caryn, watch yourself." She cut her eyes at me for only a split second, then looked away just as quickly. "May I be excused, please?"

"Why can't you stay down here and eat with everyone?"

"I have cramps," she announced without flinching.

My one hand that rested on my lap balled into a tight fist. This girl was trying my last nerves. "Was that necessary?" I asked, careful to keep my tone low and even.

"I was just telling you, Mom."

"Bye, Caryn," I spat. She wasted no time getting up

from her seat and headed for her room. "I'm sorry, Jaxon," I said, unable to look at him right that second.

"It's no problem."

We finished dinner with strained conversation, trying to make the atmosphere more comfortable, but it wasn't really working. I ended up switching on the big-screen television and letting Doug and Carrie Heffernan from *The King of Queens* pick up the tension, although it wasn't the best programming for my son. In minutes we found ourselves chuckling a bit.

After dinner CJ climbed the stairs for his nightly bath, and Jaxon and I cleaned the kitchen. I washed while he dried.

"So what is really going on with Caryn?" he asked.

"I don't know, Jaxon. I mean, I know, but I don't know. Cade's death was hard on all of us. I guess she's acting out of her pain." I didn't dare tell him about her sexual misconduct.

"Other than her attitude, what else is she doing?"

"She's just . . . she's just really acting up in school."

"Do you think she's seeking attention?" What was he, a counselor or something? My evening had been bad enough, I didn't need him playing twenty questions. Not tonight.

"I don't know what to think, to be honest with you, Jaxon," I replied, shaking my head, hoping he would leave well enough alone. He didn't.

"Maybe you should get her some counseling. I can refer you to a couple of people if you'd like."

"How do you know them?"

"My sister is a counselor at the Center for Child

and Family Services, Inc., in Hampton. I can give you her number if you want."

"That might be a good idea," I said, only halfway thinking about it, but I wanted him to stop pestering me. "Do you have her card?" Without giving a verbal response, he reached for his wallet, flicked a card from one of its folds and extended it toward me. "Just post it on the refrigerator," I said, motioning with my head. "My hands are wet."

"I hope you'll call," he said, sliding the card beneath a magnet. "You don't want to wait too long or too late."

"I won't." I led the way to the living room, inserted Tyler Perry's *Why Did I Get Married?* DVD, per Michetta's recommendation, and eased onto the sofa. Jaxon slid beside me and coaxed me into his arms.

"Janet doesn't look as young as she did on the cover of *Ebony* or *Essence* or *Jet* . . . whatever it was she was on, not too long ago," Jaxon commented, frowning. "She looking kinda old up here."

"Well, she is in her forties now. We can't stay young forever, can we?"

"No, we can't, but doggone! Guess Tyler wasn't going for all the plastic, makeup and belly exposure."

"You need to cut it out," I replied, slapping his thigh playfully.

"But you know what? She doesn't look better than you," he said in response, pecking my cheek.

"Flattery will get you everywhere." I giggled, reaching across his lap for my cordless phone. I dialed the number to the shop and waited a few seconds for an answer.

"Thank you for calling Sweet Jream's, where we're having a panty sale. This is Stephanie speaking. How can I help you?"

"Hey, it's me. How'd it go tonight?" I asked.

"We exceeded our daily goal by seven hundred dollars, our items per transaction were just a little shy of what we needed, though. We did get the floor set changed, and all the clearance items have been properly marked down. They just need to be put in size order."

"Cool. Well, don't worry about doing that tonight. I'll have Tweet take care of it in the morning. Great job tonight. Thanks so much," I ended, then settled back into Jaxon's embrace with a smile.

"Good night, Mommy. Good night, Jaxon," CJ said, running toward me with open arms, smelling like Dove soap.

"Good night, babe. Sleep tight. Don't let the bedbugs bite."

"I won't."

"Good night, man," Jaxon said, slapping hands with CJ.


I hadn't realized that I'd fallen asleep in Jaxon's arms until my cell phone started buzzing. The first thing I noticed was the time; it was just a few minutes past eleven. I shook Jaxon gently, arousing him from his dozing.

"Babe," I called softly, "it's after eleven."

He stretched upward as he unsuccessfully attempted to hold back a yawn. "Okay. Let me get my shoes on," he said sleepily. My cell phone buzzed a second time just as my home phone began to ring. "Someone really wants to get in touch with you."

"Apparently so. Hello," I spoke into the receiver.

"Is this Jream Colton?" a stoic female voice asked from the other end.

"Yes, it is."

"Ma'am, do you own Sweet Jream's, located on Town Center Drive, in Newport News?"

"Yes, what is this about?"

"Ms. Colton, this is Newport News Emergency Services. There's been a fire reported at that location. The fire department has been contacted and are there now to gain control of the situation."

My heart stopped beating as I gasped. "What!"

"There was no one reported inside the building, but the fire department is on-site to extinguish the flames, ma'am."

"Oh my, oh my, oh my," I repeated in shock. "Thank you for calling." I hung up the phone and, with a trembling voice, announced to Jaxon that my store was on fire.

"Let's go. I'll drive," he said, quickly grabbing his keys and waiting for me to shuffle into my shoes and jacket.

"I can't believe this. I just can't believe this!"

"Babe, calm down. Let's get there and see what's going on before you get too worked up."


Several blocks before we got to the store, I could smell smoke in the air and hear the sirens of fire trucks speeding in the direction of the blazes. Billows of smoke rolled up into the dark sky and hovered above our heads a full block away from the store, which is where we had to park. Jaxon normally opened my door for me, but this time I didn't wait on him. I yanked at the handle before he'd even got the truck in park and began to tear down the street, with Jaxon fast on my heels. I wasn't able to get but so close, but I covered my mouth, horrified and devastated by what I saw. My store was completely engulfed in flames. Firefighters rushed around, yelling, yanking hoses and spraying water in a manner that I'd only seen in movies. I couldn't hold back the tears as I watched all my hard work go up in smoke. Jaxon wrapped his arms tightly around me as we stood and watched in silence. Nothing could be said. Nothing at all.

Nearly two hours later, the flames were extinguished and Sweet Jream's had been utterly destroyed. There was nothing left but broken glass, blackened wood, charred clothes, melted plastic and warped racks. The store was gone, only marked by a smoking black hole.

As the firefighters wrapped up their work and slowly began to pull away, the fire marshall made his way over to me and began spewing words.

"Yeah, this was a pretty bad one here," he started, running his hand through the hair that hadn't been plastered down by sweat. "We're lucky that no lives were lost."

"What started the fire?" I asked, trying to remember if I'd seen anything in the store that looked even remotely hazardous.

"Looks like a lit cigarette was discarded in the trash can behind your counter area."

# Chapter 13

"Mrs. Colton, we are incredibly sorry for your loss, and we want to do everything we can to restore your business, but our hands, unfortunately, are tied," the insurance adjuster repeated to me for the third time. "We simply did not receive the signed documents back from you. I wish there was something we could do."

I sat on my bed in total silence for a full two hours after hanging up the phone, completely devastated. I would have cried, but I couldn't anymore. My tear ducts had been overused and dried up. How could I have been mindless, careless, stupid and irresponsible enough not to return my insurance policy? And now the store was gone. It was then that I heard the voice of the Lord speaking to me.

*"Mindless, careless, stupid and irresponsible. I remember you using those words not too long ago, Jream."*

Instantly I recalled the morning I'd taken Caryn to the store to work and continued my riot act, almost all the way there, using those same words. I knew what He would say next—tell Him the difference between the two.

My mind was so muddled, I couldn't think straight. I didn't know what to think. I didn't even want to think. What was I supposed to do now? Cade was once my passion and he was taken from me; then the store became my passion and now that was gone.

With no particular destination in mind, I got into my car, pulled onto the interstate and just drove. There were other vehicles on the road, but I didn't notice any of them. Some whizzed by me; I jetted past others in a rush to get to nowhere. From I-64, I merged right onto I-295, then a few miles later whipped onto I-95 north. For the past hour and a half, I'd been riding in silence, but I decided to switch on the radio, feeling my eyelids threaten sleep. I had to turn the volume up extra loud and sing along to keep myself alert; then I cursed myself for driving so far from home for absolutely no reason at all. I just didn't have the good sense to go back home, regardless of how emotionally drained I felt, how sleepy I was getting and how the sun was setting, paving the way for a dark night sky.

*Suppose I fell asleep behind the wheel,* I thought, glancing over at a blur of trees. *Suppose I just ran completely off. . . .*

"*Go back,*" God spoke, interrupting my insane thoughts of attempted suicide induced by drowsiness. Suddenly I was fully alert and very aware of my surroundings. I drove on for another five or so miles, contemplating what I'd heard, when I felt that strong urging again.

"*Go back.*"

This time, without question or argument, I pulled off on the next exit, circled around to the on-ramp and headed back toward home. "Might as well listen," I huffed to myself, because ignoring God was just not working out for me.

Just as I pulled back onto 64E, wondering what God had in store for me next, since he'd sent me home, I heard Him tell me to slow down. Again, without question, I obeyed. Several feet in front of me was a vehicle stopped on the side of the road, flashing its hazard lights. For some strange reason, I felt very compelled to stop and help, although I knew how dangerous it was.

"I don't know who is in that car, Lord, so protect me." I spoke aloud as I found myself depressing the brake pedal, and my hands guided the steering wheel to the side of the road. Apprehensively I got out of my car, approached the vehicle and peeked into the dark windows. A woman sat with her head leaning against the steering wheel. The rapid rising and falling of her shoulders indicated that she was crying. Softly I tapped on the window, startling her. With wide, scared eyes, she stared at me. I felt a drop in my stomach as I immediately recognized her face. Out of all the people in the entire United States of America that it could have been, it was Genevieve E. Fauntleroy . . . the "platinum contributor" who forced me out of her church pew months ago. I wanted to stomp right back to my car, but, heck, I was out there now.

"Are you okay?" I yelled over passing traffic through her closed window. She eased the window down slightly. "Are you okay? Do you need help?"

"I . . . I'm . . ." Before she could say anything else, her hands flew to her face and she sobbed even more profusely. Sympathetically I opened her car door and coaxed her from the seat with a gentle tug, guided her to the back end of her car and wrapped my arms around her. And, like a feverish, teething baby, she cried for nearly ten minutes before she pulled herself together and began wringing her hands. "Thank you for stopping. I'm okay," she mumbled unconvincingly.

"Are you sure?" I was sincerely concerned about her well-being, regardless of the fact that she'd really offended me. "I'll tell you what"—I pointed at a road sign several yards away—"we're right here at this exit. Why don't we just grab a cup of coffee or something. That will probably help you feel better." She nodded as she used the back of her hand to wipe her nose. "I'll follow you," I said, patting her back comfortingly.

Cautiously we climbed back into our vehicles, took the next off-ramp and pulled into a McDonald's parking lot. It was clear to me that I hadn't stood out in her mind as much as she had in mine. She didn't find me the least bit familiar.

Rather than just getting coffee, we ordered combo meals and sat in a far corner, nibbling on fries and nuggets.

"Thank you again for stopping for me. You didn't have to do that."

"No problem," I answered. "I didn't have any-where to be."

"I guess you're wondering why I was such a wreck back there," she started to explain, mixing extra cream into her cup. She kept her eyes diverted for several seconds.

"I'm here to listen if you'd like to talk."

With a sigh, she began pouring out her heart. "I'd just left a doctor's office up in Richmond to get a third opinion." She paused as she wiped away a trickling tear. "I've been diagnosed with breast cancer and they are telling me I need to start chemo right away."

"I'm so very sorry to hear that," I offered, remembering how hurt I was when Cade got that same diagnosis on his lungs.

"Thanks"—she sniffed—"right now, I'm just confused and—and devastated. I can't believe that this is happening to me. I've been incredibly fatigued and depressed and just don't know what to do."

I didn't know what I should have been saying, but it was uncomfortably odd that I had absolutely no response, so I said the first thing that popped into my head after whispering a quick prayer for God's help, since He had directed me to stop. "Do you have a support system to help you through?"

"I have my husband and kids. I guess they offer some comfort, but not really."

"What about friends?"

"I don't have any," she said, almost whining as she shook her head. "I'm so stupid. You wouldn't believe how ugly I've treated people in the past." *Oh yes, I would!* I thought, but I kept it to myself. "Just treating people any kind of way, looking down my nose at them, thinking I was better and above." Genevieve dug in a raspberry-colored Marc Jacobs purse for a tissue much softer than the napkin she'd used a minute before to wipe her nose. "I've been a fool," she muttered.

"Have you researched any support groups? I'm sure there are some in your local area."

"Not really. I've been spending more time in denial than focusing on healing and support, but I guess it's time for me to face the music," she ended sadly.

"Well, with today's technology, I'm sure you will be fine. There are treatments and procedures that have helped thousands of women survive," I said knowingly, although I didn't really have a clue as to what I was talking about.

*"Tell her that this sickness will not lead her to death, but it's for My glory."*

With a heart full of compassion, I obeyed, repeating to her exactly what God had spoken to me. Then I said something that slipped from my lips before I realized it and shocked me. "You know, God is a healer and all you need to do is just believe in Him for your healing." Internally I gasped. Where had that come from, and how could I have said that, when God had turned His back on me when I believed in Him for Cade's health to be restored?

She nodded. "I appreciate you saying that. Pray that I'll have the faith." I crossed my fingers beneath the table, hoping that she wasn't expecting me to pray for her right there, on the spot. "Would you mind praying for me? You seem like such a woman of faith."

*Who me? I'm not even speaking to God right now!* "Sure," I agreed. Nervously I cleared my throat as she reached across the table for my hands and bowed her head. "Father God, we come boldly before your throne seeking your mercy and your grace in this situation. Lord, we know you hold healing in your hands, for you are the Lord, our God, who heals us from all of our diseases. While I know that you will heal Genevieve, give her the faith to believe you and give her the strength to stand on your promises. Encourage and strengthen her daily, and may you get the glory out of this situation. In Jesus' name I pray, amen."

"Amen," she mumbled through tears. Together we stood and she hugged me long and tightly. Once she loosened her embrace, we cleared the table, then headed for our cars. "I can't say thank you enough," she exclaimed, now wearing a smile, though weakened by her crying.

"You're welcome," I said. "You be encouraged and take care of yourself." We both got in our cars and she patiently waited for me to back out first. Just before I pulled off, she leapt from her car, a look of surprise on her face, as she yelled, "Hey! How did you know my name?"

As though I'd not heard her, I pulled onto the road and sped away, leaving her awestruck in the parking lot.

The last hour I'd spent with Genevieve surprised me, uncovering my thoughts about God's healing hidden deep in my own heart. I couldn't explain why He'd allowed Cade to die, but I did know that He was still God and He was Sovereign. Now that I was alone again, thoughts of my own problems began to push Genevieve and her situation from my mind. My store was still gone, there was no insurance coverage and now I didn't have a job. I didn't know what to do. Really, there was nothing I could do.

I drove the rest of the way home in silence, reminded of a million chores that needed my attention, that I suddenly had the time to take care of. When I walked in, Caryn stood at the sink, washing dishes with her iPod headphones over her ears, and I could hear the swishing and whirring of the washing machine. Caryn hadn't noticed me as I walked through the kitchen toward the staircase. The living room was in perfect order—smelled like lemon-fresh furniture polish—and tracks left by the vacuum cleaner were visible in the carpet. I tiptoed upstairs, peeked in CJ's room, where he was already tucked in bed, then went to my own room, fell across my bed and dialed Jaxon.

"I've been worried sick about you," he exclaimed when he answered. "I've been calling you all day and no one knew where you were."

"I know. I'm sorry. I just needed to clear my head and didn't feel much like talking to anyone."

"Are you all right?"

"I guess. I could be worse, right?"

"You could always be worse." He paused momentarily. "So what did you do today?"

"I think I saved some woman's life."

"Wow! That's something that doesn't happen every day. Tell me about it." I summarized my past few hours, probably in more detail than Jaxon cared to hear. When I finished, I could tell by his tone he was smiling. "Look at my baby being a Good Samaritan! Stopping by the side of the road to help a complete stranger."

"Well, she wasn't exactly a complete stranger," I replied, then explained our first meeting. "She didn't recognize me at all, though. Which I can understand why—she barely looked at me that day."

"That makes the story even better, babe. To see past that and still help her? Like I said, you were being a Good Samaritan."

"I guess you could call it that," I said meekly. "I reckon I'll get off this phone and get some laundry done. I'll call you in a little bit."

"Okay, babe. Love you."

"Love you too," I ended.

I emptied my hamper, gathered an armful of white clothes and headed downstairs, no longer seeing Caryn, who had retreated to her bedroom. After starting the washer again, filled with my own clothes, I pulled a mug from the cabinet and fixed myself a cup of hot chocolate while I thought back on Stephanie's profuse and repeated apology. No amount of saying "I'm sorry" would bring my store back . . . especially when she shouldn't have been smoking in the store in the first place. I serious[ly] considered suing her for damages; I didn't care [if] took her fifty years to pay me back. My att[orney] would be able to advise me, once I called hi[m] morning. Grabbing a legal pad, I began lis[ting ques]tions to ask, until I heard the washing [machine do] its work.

Normally, Caryn was pretty thoro[ugh with] her laundry, but she'd apparently [

load of clothes in the dryer. I folded up several pairs of her jeans, along with a few T-shirts, and took them up to her room, where the door was shut.

There was no such thing as an off-limits room in my house, so without thought I twisted the knob of her bedroom door, eased it open not to disturb her sleeping and tiptoed inside. Her room was in perfect order, with everything in its place as usual. She lay sprawled across her bed, in a sea of scattered note-book paper, pen still in hand and lamp still on. I set the clothes on her bean bag, then tiptoed over to turn her light off after taking a sneak peek at her creative expression. When I did that, I got the shock of my life:

*Dear Daddy,*

*I miss you so much and life here without you is just miserable. It really is the pits, Daddy. It's like I don't know what to do with my life any-more and sometimes I don't even feel like living.*

*Mom is so mad at me that I think she stopped loving me, although I did do something really bad in school. I got caught kinda fooling around in the boys' bathroom. That's what started it all. I'm ashamed of myself, Daddy. I did expect Mom to be mad when she found out, but I didn't think she would just totally stop speaking to me forever. She has barely said a word to me in months and that really hurts. She talks to CJ and she even has a boyfriend now. (He's okay, by the way.) She talks to them ll the time.*

*I know if you were here, you would be angry*

*too. You probably are angry at me from where
you are, but you would still love me, wouldn't
you? I wish I could come where you are. Before
you died, you told me that you didn't want me to
cry too long when you died because for you to
be absent in the body was to be present with
God the Father. If I am absent from my body,
maybe I will get to see you, my father, again. I
think about that every day. I know that being
with you would be much better than being here.
Especially since Mom doesn't love me anymore.
I think I might*

Her writing ended there. I stood frozen in place
for what seemed like hours, but in reality I stood
perfectly still for two minutes. When I did finally
find the strength to move, I fell to my knees, right
there at my daughter's bedside, crying silent tears.
Gently I rested my hand on Caryn's arm and stared
at her restful repose, wondering what she was
dreaming. As quietly as I could, I gathered her
papers to the side, then crawled into her bed and
draped my arm around her. She stirred slightly, rec-
ognizing my presence.

"Mom?" she mumbled in her muddled, confused
daze of sleep.

"Shhh . . ." I ran my hand over her silky locks of
hair, which she'd not tied up before drifting off to
sleep. I held her silently, hoping that she'd sense my
love for her through my embrace.

I lay there for the better part of an hour, then
kissed her forehead and slowly pulled away after
whispering in her ear that I loved her.

Once I got in my bedroom, I guess I found myself laying into God.

"You took Cade. My store has burned to the ground. And now you're gonna snatch my daughter too?" I hurled. "You're just going to sit on high and let my baby take her life?"

*"I wasn't going to let her—You were going to,"* He answered softly.

"Excuse me? Aren't you the one in control and stuff?"

*"Jream, I instructed you weeks ago to speak to your daughter in love. Did you do it? Did you obey me?"*

That shut me right on up. I bit into my bottom lip, remembering the day I heard Him tell me to go tell Caryn that I loved her and I dismissed His instruction. He said one more thing to me that night:

*"Every wise woman builds her house, but a foolish woman tears it down with her own hands."*

# Chapter 14

After locking myself in my bedroom in complete silence and meditation for three days, I was ready to ask my daughter's forgiveness. Before I did, I slid out of my bed that morning and onto my knees and began to pray like I hadn't in a long time. Through tears I repented for my stubbornness, my hardheadedness, my bitterness and every other "ness" that I could think of. I repented for my lack of reverence and my anger, knowing that God was and had always been the answer.

Then I thanked Him for His loving kindness and His tender mercies that had been made new to me every morning. I thanked Him for not cutting me off when I rebelled against Him, and for never treating me the way I'd treated my daughter. I realized how hypocritical I'd been in not speaking to Him, while practically cursing my daughter under my breath when she was silent toward me. I thanked Him for Jaxon and for thinking enough of me to send a man that truly, truly loved me in ways I never thought possible. I never thought I'd be able to love again, but somehow, someway, God had restored my broken heart like only He would be able to do. I smiled just thinking of Jaxon while I prayed.

"And one last thing, Lord," I continued. "Guide our footsteps as you continue to bring restoration to this household."

"Caryn," I called softly from her doorway.

"Yes," she mumbled from beneath her covers.

"Wake up, sweetie. I need to talk to you."

"Okay." Slowly she pushed her covers away and sat up, looking around her bedroom sleepily. "What day is it?"

"Saturday, babe. Come on, we're going out to breakfast." Her eyebrows shot up in surprise.

"Okay?" she questioned. "What's going on?"

"Nothing, we just need to spend some time together so I can tell you some things."

Thirty minutes later, she met me downstairs with her purse on her shoulder. "I'm ready."

"Do you have anyplace in particular you'd like to go?"

"I get to pick the place?"

"Sure."

"Ummm . . . how about IHOP?"

"IHOP, it is." I waltzed to the den where Jaxon and CJ were entertaining themselves with the Wii console, playing a game that required them to stand up and dance. "All right, we'll be back."

"Bye," they both huffed, jumping and twisting, but never looking over at me.

Seated across from me in a booth, Caryn ordered

a three-egg western omelet. I chose three buttermilk pancakes topped with strawberries and whipped cream. While we waited on our meals, I started my apology.

"Caryn, I want to first tell you that I love you very, very much. I know I haven't acted like it lately, especially when you got in trouble at school, and for that, I ask you to forgive me." I paused, not really expecting her to comment or accept at that point. "I guess when your dad died, I didn't think of anyone but myself, wallowing in my own sorrows and misery. When I looked at you and CJ, I knew you were hurting, but you seemed to be doing just fine, and I took that for granted. I was too consumed with my own pain." Caryn's eyes began to fill with tears, which spilled over seconds later. "I haven't nurtured you properly and given you the love you needed," I admitted shamefully. "But if you'll let me, I'd like to begin." Caryn slid from her side of the booth and came over to my side, throwing her arms around me and burying her face in my chest. Just then, the server walked up with our food, but I motioned her away by quickly shaking my head, as neither of us was fit to eat right that second.

"I love you, Mommy," she mumbled.

"I love you too."

We held each other for a few minutes longer; then somehow we pulled ourselves together and were able to begin our meals. I shared with her that I thought it would help her to see a counselor and discuss her feelings about losing her father; to which she nodded, although she kept her eyes downward on her plate.

"And I want you to know that I am here for you. To listen when you need me to, and to support you. I don't want you to feel condemned by your mistakes, or feel like I'm judging you, okay?"

"Okay," Caryn uttered in shame.

"We are going to learn and grow from our past mistakes. The both of us." She nodded, still not looking up. "Caryn, look at me." When our eyes met, I continued. "I love you," I said adamantly. "Don't forget that."

"I won't."

After breakfast we spent the day shopping and pampering ourselves with pedicures, manicures and brow waxes. I called a couple of times to check on the boys, who seemed to be doing just fine.

"CJ and I have a surprise for you two when you get back. Call me when you're on the way," Jaxon requested.

"A surprise like what? Like my house is still in one piece?"

"Hardy-har-har. A surprise like I'm not telling you, because then it wouldn't be a surprise, smarty-pants," he teased. "Just call me when you're on your way," he concluded.

Caryn and I went one more place before heading home, which was to my belly-dancing class. She was shocked and amazed at how fluid I was in performing the movements.

"Mom, you look like Shakira and Beyoncé in that video for 'Beautiful Liar'!" She gawked as she tried to get her hip rotations down. Together we twisted, hip rolled, snaked our arms and shuffled our knees, hardly paying the instructor any attention, but enjoying each other instead. We decided by the end of the class that we'd continue attending the sessions together in our new commitment to have consistent mother/daughter time.

When Caryn and I did get home, CJ and Jaxon stood dressed in black at the dining-room table, which had been set for two and held glowing candlesticks. Both of them had a white towel draped across their arms.

"Goo-deeve-ning, mah-dom," Jaxon said, sounding more like the Count from *Sesame Street* than anything else. Caryn and I couldn't help but snicker when CJ repeated Jaxon in the same attempted accent. "Please have a seat," Jaxon added, pulling out a chair for me, while CJ did the same for his sister.

"We need to go out more often," I commented, impressed by their efforts.

Giggling all the way, CJ darted for the kitchen and reappeared seconds later, presenting Caryn with a bowl of fresh Bibb lettuce tossed with toasted walnuts, red onions and blue cheese dressing, followed by Jaxon serving me.

"Enjoy your salads, ladies," CJ said, bowing. Like hired help, they both went into the kitchen and stayed hidden for fifteen minutes, then returned with plates of chicken rigatoni with mushrooms and caramelized onions.

"Mmm," I moaned, filling my mouth with a forkful. "This is really good! You cook too? I'm going to have to think about keeping you around!"

"We didn't actually—"

Jaxon cut CJ off with a nervous chuckle. "CJ, you forgot the bread, man! How'd you forget the bread?"

"Oh yeah!" he piped.

"So you didn't cook this, huh?"

"Baby, what's important is that you, the queen, and you, the princess," he said, looking at Caryn, "enjoy your food."

"I don't know about Mom, but I'm definitely enjoying mine! This is awesome."

They tried to serve us huge slices of chocolate cake, but being stuffed to the gills, I couldn't eat another bite. When I did push back from the table, I felt like I was about ready to deliver a baby. Caryn thanked Jaxon and CJ, stood to her feet and gathered her bags from just inside the door.

"Thanks for a great day, Mom," she said, pecking me on the cheek. "I'm going to bring my things up."

"You're welcome, honey."

I waddled to the living room and propped my feet up on the coffee table. CJ immediately came and removed my shoes.

"At your service," he said, bowing.

"Thank you, sir." I nodded.

"Can I go play Wii again?" CJ asked, looking at Jaxon.

"Take the trash out first, man," Jaxon instructed as he swung my feet off the coffee table and onto his lap.

"Yes, sir." CJ saluted, then ran out.

"So how'd it go?" Jaxon asked, kneading my right foot with his thumbs.

"We had a great day, I think," I replied, nodding. "I, ummm . . . shared some things from my heart. We agreed to get her in counseling, and had a good time shopping. It's a start to a long road of healing. How about you? How was your day? I guess you spent it slaving over a hot stove, huh?"

"Something like that," he said, grinning.

"Mmm-hmm. Thank you so much, babe, it was delicious."

"My pleasure."

"And you massage feet. I think you're a keeper," I said, wiggling my toes in Jaxon's lap.

"Well, you're really going to be ready to marry me when I get in here and wash these dishes." He snickered as he transferred my feet to the couch and walked into the kitchen.

Caryn was already up and dressed by the time I showered, dressed, made it downstairs, clad modestly in a pair of jeans and a sweater. I walked over to her and kissed her cheek. "Good morning, sweetheart," I said lovingly.

"Good morning."

"You ready?"

She nodded with a smile. "Yes, ma'am."

"'Ma'am'? When did you start that?" I asked, swatting at her behind. She giggled as she jerked out of my way.

My stomach jumped a bit when we pulled in front of the building where Jaxon's sister, Dr. Jamillah Sutton, worked. We agreed to meet with her, but thought it best to get a referral from Dr. Sutton rather than have Caryn be seen by her, due to Caryn's apprehension in thinking that Jaxon might press her for private information.

"We're here to see Dr. Sutton," I said to the receptionist. She confirmed our appointment and names, then asked us to have a seat. Minutes later a petite woman with beautiful coconut-brown skin and a headful of shiny two-strand twists came out to greet us.

"Ms. Colton? Hi, I'm Jamillah Sutton," she said, extending her hand. The family resemblance was striking.

"Nice to meet you."

"Likewise. Jaxon has spoken very highly of you. And you must be Caryn."

"Yes, ma'am." Caryn nodded as she stood to her feet.

"Come on back," she offered, escorting us to her office. "Now, I understand that my brother, Jaxon, referred you to me for a referral."

"Yes, that's right. We experienced the loss of my husband, and Caryn's father, about a year and a half ago, and it's been a struggle for us all."

"I understand. The loss of a loved one is always difficult and you have my sympathy."

"Thank you," Caryn and I said in unison.

"And it's important that you heal properly from the tragedy," she added. "Well, per your request, I won't be seeing you personally, but I can refer you to my esteemed and trusted colleague. I'll be glad to walk you down to her office. She's expecting you." We rose to our feet and followed her down a hallway, where she tapped twice, then poked her head in the door. "Hey, I'm here with the Coltons," she said, widening the door.

Caryn and I entered the room to come face-to-face

with Dr. Genevieve E. Fauntleroy. She was already standing, but her hands flew to her face and covered her mouth when she saw me.

"Oh, my goodness! It's you!" she exclaimed.

"You two have met before?" Jaxon's sister asked.

"Yes!" Genevieve shrieked. "Oh, my goodness, yes!"

"It's good to see you," I stated calmly while Dr. Sutton exited quietly. Caryn's eyes bounced back and forth between me and Genevieve as she came around her desk and threw her arms around me.

"I've been praying every night that God would let me run into you one more time so I could thank you. I will never forget what you did for me. And you know what?" Before she could continue, I asked Caryn to wait out in the hall. I didn't think it would be exactly fitting for her to see the counselor potentially breaking down. Once Caryn left, and the door closed behind her, Genevieve continued. "As I was saying, I had been praying about you and asking God to lead me to you, but not only that, He . . . He brought to my memory where we first met," she said, her voice beginning to tremble. "And how I treated you so terribly with my nasty attitude. Please forgive me. I am truly, truly sorry. The nerve of me, asking you to move out of *my* seat," she huffed, emphasizing the word by making quotation marks with her fingers. "I was so stuck on myself, it's a wonder God didn't slap me down, right in the middle of the church." She shook her head at her own audacity. "That's how you knew my name. And you were still gracious enough to help me that night. I don't know what I would have done, had you not stopped."

"Well, how is your health?"

"I'm coming along." She nodded, with a doleful look. "I'm doing my best to hold on to my faith."

"Good, good."

"Enough about me." She waved. "How are you doing?"

"Good," I answered semihonestly. "Just trying to work through some things."

"We all have things that we need to work through," she said humbly. "And God is just teaching me more and more each day how to truly lean on and trust in Him. You know, I thought I had a relationship with Him before, but when I got that diagnosis, and went into crises, He showed me myself." She paused, shaking her head shamefully. "I was a wretch undone. Then I had gotten so angry with God that I just said I wasn't going to deal with Him anymore." She reminded me of myself. "I didn't want to hear anything He had to say. Oh, I'd go to church and give to the ministry and attend Bible study and all of that, but I didn't want anything to do with God." She snatched a tissue from a box on her desk and dabbed at her eyes. "I'm sorry. I know you didn't come here for this. You came to get help from me, but here I am crying on your shoulder . . . again."

"It's all right," I assured her, feeling myself teetering on the brink of unleashed emotions.

"Anyway, that night that I was driving home, I had challenged God to prove Himself to me. I was such a wreck that I couldn't even see straight down the road. So I pulled over and said, 'God, if you be God like you say you are, then let somebody stop for me, and I don't mean stop and just see that I'm all right.

Let them show me your love in their actions.' I even had the nerve to give him only ten minutes," she said, chuckling. "Like He's my butler or something! I was just above myself with arrogance! It's a wonder He didn't strike me down dead. But, anyway, He was down to one minute, and trust me, I was counting the seconds, and right before you knocked on the window, I heard Him clear as a bell say, *'I am the Lord that healeth thee from all thy diseases.'* So when you stopped for me that night and let me cry in your arms, sat with me, listened to me, even prayed with me . . . I knew it was nobody but God." She handed me a tissue as we both smiled and cried in awe at God's amazing way of making things happen . . . of being in control.

Genevieve pulled herself together after profusely thanking me again, then called Caryn in to begin her counseling appointment. With skill, grace and love, she urged Caryn to discuss her feelings and emotions, to share from her heart. I stayed and held her hand, handed her tissues and leaned her head against my shoulder when she needed me; and I left the room a couple of times per Caryn's request.

While I stood in the hallway, I found myself smiling at God, thankful for His mercy and grace.

# Chapter 15

It had seemed a bit odd at first, but Genevieve had asked me to escort her to a few of her doctor's appointments. I decided to see past my own selfish discomforts and be there for someone else.

"I'll be glad to go with you," I answered the day she called me in tears, needing support. I drove to her home to pick her up, once she stated that she felt somewhat weary. She took a seat in the car and exhaled as if she'd just finished climbing ten flights of stairs. I couldn't picture myself being in her shoes, and could only imagine what it was like to be experiencing such an ordeal. Wishing there were something I could do, I rested my hand on top of hers and she smiled weakly. Words weren't necessary.

Since I no longer had the store to keep me busy, I became Genevieve's nutritionist, going to her house nearly every morning and making sure she put the right foods in her body that would promote healing. Sometimes she would cry and say that I was fussing over her too much, but I paid her absolutely no mind. While both our kids were in school, and her husband was away at work, I prepared her breakfast, lunch and dinner, and made sure that she had proper snacks including nutritional drinks and freshly made juices. Even though she'd started her chemotherapy treatments, most days instead of being completely fatigued and depressed, she was able to hold on to some energy and stay in good spirits.

Once her family got home in the evenings, I would go home and see after my own family. I went back to cooking dinner every night, focusing on the kids' favorites. I created themed nights during the week for us to spend quality time together, including game night, movie night, craft night, family talk night and even Bible study night. We had begun attending church regularly with Jaxon, and the kids got involved with the auxiliary departments right away. With her beautiful voice, Caryn joined the youth choir, and CJ was in a mentoring program geared toward developing young men into Godly men. He was elated to have Jaxon as his mentor.

Tonight was family talk night, and I needed to discuss with the kids that I'd have to look for work soon. Our home had been paid for in Cade's passing, and there were resources in the bank, but it had been dwindling away since the shop burned down. The Fauntleroys had several times offered to pay me as a caregiver for Genevieve, but I wouldn't hear of it. I hadn't quite decided what I wanted to do, but one thing was for certain—I had to do something soon.

Jaxon rang the doorbell just as I placed a large bowl of spaghetti and meatballs on the table, along with a dish of steamed broccoli with cheese and toasted garlic bread.

"Hey, love," he stated, pecking me on the cheek and offering me a bouquet of yellow tulips. He always brought flowers to dinner. Always.

"Hey, you're just in time." I smiled. "Kids, dinner's ready." While we waited for Caryn and CJ, Jaxon gathered me in his arms and kissed me passionately.

"I love you, Jream," he whispered.

"I love you too," I returned. CJ's giggles had us pull back from each other. "Nosy," I teased, playfully slapping his head as he walked past us.

When we were all seated, CJ to my left, Caryn to my right, and Jaxon across from me, we joined hands and Jaxon said grace.

"So whose starting tonight?" I asked. Caryn started, expressing how she'd initiated a few conversations with her guidance counselor about college. That was definitely a money topic.

"She said that she was going to start putting some application packages together for me to review," Caryn continued.

"Where is it that you think you might want to go?" Jaxon asked.

"I'm not really sure right now, because I just started seriously thinking about it. I'm hoping this summer I can do some campus tours or something that will give me an idea of the schools' cultures, ethnic mixes and study programs."

"Good idea. You know Regent University is my alma mater," he stated proudly. "I think they have a performing arts program."

"No, I want to focus more on business, management development, and stuff like that," she replied, winding noodles around her fork. "Maybe one day Mom and I can get the store back open."

"Sounds like a plan," he agreed.

"Speaking of the store, I'm going to have to start looking for work soon," I announced. "Especially if you want to go to college, Caryn."

"Are you going to work at another store, Mom?" CJ asked.

"I'm not sure yet." Another store would probably be the easiest and best place for me to go, but I struggled with the thought, wishing I could have Sweet Jream's back again. "I just wanted to let you guys know I probably won't be sitting at home much longer." The table fell silent as we devoured more of our meal.

"Well, I want to get your kids' thoughts on something," Jaxon announced. "Who do you think is the most beautiful woman in the world?"

"My mom!" CJ answered right away. Caryn waited to see what Jaxon was getting at.

"Do you think we make a good couple?"

"I think you look great together," Caryn offered.

"Your mom is the best thing that's ever happened to me." He nodded. "And I want you two to hear it from me, that I love her very much."

"I heard you say that when you came in the door and y'all were kissing." CJ giggled.

"And when you love someone, you take the time and make the effort to tell them," Jaxon stated, looking directly at me. "I love you, Jream," he said, a second time, causing me to blush in front of the kids.

"I love you too." It was hard to say that in front of the kids, but I'd said it, and it felt good.

# Chapter 16

Over the next eight months, Caryn did a complete turnaround in her behavior. I'd ended up transferring her to another school, not wanting the shame and guilt of her past to plague her for the rest of her high-school days. She still had a year and a half to go. She faithfully kept her counseling appointments, privately working out her frustration, disappointments and hurts with a different counselor that Genevieve had recommended. Some of the sessions I was allowed to take part in, while others were completely confidential. Each time Caryn went, I prayed for her and with her, wrapped my arms around her and whispered that I loved her in her ear.

Genevieve kept her doctor's appointments and experienced God's hand of healing as her cancer went into remission. And over that course of time, she and I became great friends, often chatting about God's goodness over a cup of coffee at Starbucks.

Even though we'd spent the past several months together, I had never mentioned to Genevieve that I'd once owned Sweet Jream's. I'd always made our time spent together all about her and getting her well. I suppose, this one particular day, I just felt like sharing, and made mention that I missed running the store.

"What store?" she asked. Once she found out that I'd owned the shop, and how it had been lost, she blew me totally away.

"Let's go," she ordered, gulping down the last mouthful of a frappe latte.

"Go where?" Genevieve was already tugging me by my arm, out of my chair and into her car.

"We're going to the bank."

"To the bank? For what?" I asked confused.

"God is about to bless your socks off!" She pulled out her cell phone and dialed her husband. "Hey, sweetheart . . . good! Listen, hon. I figured out why we haven't been able to lease that space in Jefferson Commons," she said, referencing a newly developed retail shopping center, where she and her husband owned a building. "It already has someone else's name on it." As she filled her husband in on what she meant, my heart stopped beating, listening to her explain to him that she was giving me the property. *Giving* it to me! Not leasing, not selling, she was actually signing the property over to me.

"Genevieve," I tried to interrupt, but she shushed me with a wave of her hand.

"Un-uh. I don't want to hear it, Jream. You just don't know what you did for me that night. This store has been sitting vacant for over a year now, and we couldn't even give it away, no matter how inexpensively we tried to lease or sell it. And now I know exactly why," she ended, pulling her auto into the bank. "Follow me."

Together we entered the bank, her in confidence and me in disbelief. She talked with one of the account services representatives for several minutes, then handed me a cashier's check large enough to fully restock and reopen my store.

"I can't take this, Gen!" I said, holding my hands in my lap.

"Yes, you can, and yes, you will! If you don't do anything else ever again in your life, you are going to take this check and get your store back up!"

I couldn't believe it. Just like that, in the snap of a finger, Sweet Jream's was reopened and my staff was back . . . with the exception of Stephanie. Although I forgave her, I wasn't going to be the same fool twice. I even dropped the pending lawsuit against her for damages, for which she did write me a letter, both apologizing and thanking me over and over again.

Even Caryn asked to be on staff, expressing how she wanted to learn the ropes and position herself to work alongside me and open future stores after she finished college. She had even begun helping me build a Web presence with an online store at www.sweetjreams.com. She put her computer skills to use and spent many days after school performing online marketing tasks, driving customers to the site, sending out e-newsletters and processing orders.

Tweet was able to have her bridal shower at Sweet Jream's, the weekend before the *second* grand reopening, and two weeks before her wedding. Her friends and family bought so much merchandise for

Tweet that I had to process a rush order to make sure we'd be set for the influx of customers we'd get the following week. Their purchases made a great jump start for the company's bottom line.

Once the store did open, no longer would Sweet Jream's be open on Sundays.

Jaxon and I sat together, hand in hand, in the midst of Tweet's other guests. I had never in my life seen such a beautiful wedding as the Johnson/Percy union in holy matrimony. Tweet themed her wedding "The Golden Commitment" and decorated the church in varied shades of gold, copper and bronze. She'd purchased several strings of gold Christmas lights and had them attached to the underside of the pews in the sanctuary, which created an incredible golden glow from beneath the seats. Copper tulle draped each pew, embellished with beautiful golden cross ornaments alternated with gold-and-rhinestone *P* initial ornaments. Elaborate flower arrangements lined a short flight of stairs that led up to the pulpit. Golden columns draped with the same copper tulle and gold flowers marked the place where she would take her vows.

Thirty minutes prior to the wedding's start, Brian McKnight, Luther Vandross, Boyz II Men, Eric Benet and Babyface helped everyone understand exactly what it was that Alonzo felt for the woman he was making his wife. As the ceremony opened, a moving hymnal medley, played by Titus Pollard from his *Conversation with a Psalmist* CD, introduced the entrance of the officiator and the bride and groom's parents. While Titus masterfully tickled the keys of his piano, a low whisper began to circulate around the sanctuary, because Alonzo had not yet taken his place. I giggled to myself as I watched the heads turn and eyes dart around to every corner of the church in search of the groom.

As soon as the parents had been comfortably seated, the music changed as a songstress stood before a microphone and began singing Chrisette Michele's "Is This the Way Love Feels?" With mesmerizing power and soul, she sang the lyrics as the ladies Tweet had designated as "women of honor" slowly proceeded down the aisle, dressed in champagne halter dresses, with bouquets created from golden roses, escorted by handsome groomsmen. Just as the last couple stepped into their place, the musicians and soloist came down from the song's powerful climax, falling nearly silent, with the exception of a few soulful chords and the tap on the hi-hat cymbals. That was when Alonzo made his entrance, causing the audience to applaud with surprise. The expression on his face was priceless as he took a gentlemanly stroll to his position, with a grin that could only say he was having the best day of his life. He took his place alongside the officiator, then signaled the ushers to pull out the aisle runner, preparing for his bride's entrance.

Quickly the first soloist left the stage and was replaced by a couple that sang Chrisette Michele's "Golden" as a duet. During the musical intro, the back doors of the church opened, revealing Tweet standing in the doorway in a stunning gold gown with intricate beading and sequins. The mermaid fit showcased her perfect figure, and an exquisite golden tiara caught every ray of light in the room, giving the illusion that she was walking in, escorted by the morning sun. On the arm of her father, she gracefully floated toward her groom as a fifteen-foot chiffon train trailed behind her, its ends carried by her twin niece and nephew. As the female soloist sang the second verse, asking the groom to be the man of her dreams, get down on one knee and propose, Alonzo did just that. He dropped to one knee, and in awe of her beauty, he had to wipe a few tears away with a handkerchief. As a matter of fact, several people patted at their eyes, including me. Once Tweet was close enough, Alonzo took her hand and stood to his feet while the duet closed the song, and shortly after, they exchanged vows.

With love-filled words and commitments, they slid rings onto each other's fingers, but nothing had prepared us for what happened next. Alonzo again dropped to a single knee as he dug in his pocket and signaled two of Tweet's "women of honor" to come to her side.

"Teresa," he began, "since the day I first laid eyes on you, I fell in love with you so completely. You have been more than I could have ever even dreamed I wanted in a woman, a friend, a lover and a wife. I love you from the crown you wear on your head to the beautiful toes on your feet." At that, Tweet leaned on the two women beside her while Alonzo carefully coaxed her to lift her foot, removed her golden stiletto and placed a toe ring on her fourth toe. The audience gasped in amazement while Tweet trembled and cried.

Alonzo took his time refastening her shoe, then stood again for the Communion and prayer portion of the ceremony. As the couple opened the small portions of crackers and juice, partook, then knelt for prayer, on the left side of the altar, a young woman dressed in loose-fitting jeans and a crisp white shirt stood to face a huge five-foot-by-four-foot canvas. As Fred Hammond's "Draw Nigh" played in the background, the young woman began to quickly cover the canvas with black paint, making swirls of nothing at all, but by the time the song ended, the canvas had been transformed into a painting of Tweet resting against Alonzo's chest, while he gazed upward as if seeking direction from and expressing gratitude to God. Tissue after tissue was being pulled from Kleenex boxes all over the sanctuary. Jaxon draped his arm around my shoulders and gave me a protective and loving squeeze.

"I love you, Jream," he whispered.

My words were so slurred and mumbled from having been moved to tears, I'm not even sure what I said to him, although I was trying to say, "I love you too, Jaxon."

We'd not even noticed that there had been no unity candles in place until the next part of the ceremony when the officiator began speaking again. On a small table sat a tall clear apothecary jar partially filled with clear glass beads. Beside it were two smaller golden jars with lids

"This jar," the preacher began, "symbolizes the lives of these two individuals, Teresa Johnson and Alonzo Percy, coming together as one. If you notice, in this jar, there are clear stones in its bottom, symbolizing the clear need to have the

Lord as a foundation upon which this marriage will be able to stand." A quiet hush of "ah" rose from the audience. "Both of these smaller jars hold sand, representing the fine and intricate facets of both these lives. Their gifts, their talents, their unique characteristics and even their flaws and short-comings." Together Tweet and Alonzo lifted their jars and began to pour gold sand and champagne-colored sand, making a unique pattern of circles and waves, which formed against the glass. "As they pour this sand from each of their jars into this one jar, these sands never can and will be separated again, and in as much, we believe their love for one another will meld them together to be inseparable."

Just when we thought we could take no more, the officiator gave permission for Alonzo to kiss the bride. Immediately Etta James's "At Last" began to play. They kissed long and passionately, Alonzo gathering her more and more into his arms; then they began to slowly dance right there on the pulpit, as if there were not a single other soul in the room.


As we all left the wedding for the reception, there was no doubt that we all had been reminded of the hypnotizing power of love. "That was awe-some," I said to Jaxon as we rode to the reception, discussing our favorite and most awe-filled parts of the ceremony.

"Yes, it was. I've never seen anything like it. Maybe one day that will be us." He reached over and patted my leg, smiling. I rested my hand atop of his and leaned over a bit to kiss him.

Once the dance party started up, Jaxon and I took the floor and did every dance we possibly could without embarrassing ourselves. Tweet started the party with the Electric Slide, transitioned to a *Soul Train* line, and it was on from there. Circling, kicking and spinning with Jaxon, I laughed like I hadn't in years. Just as Mary J. ended "Just Fine," an instrumental of Brian McKnight's "Love of My Life" began to play.

"Come on, babe, I need some water or something." I giggled. I tugged at Jaxon's arm, ready to sit down for a few, but he resisted, looking intently into my eyes. And like in a dream, he slid to one knee and produced a ring seemingly from thin air, and held it up for me to see while someone slipped a cordless microphone into his hand. In the most amazing falsetto voice I'd ever heard, Jaxon sang to me how wonderful, amazing and incredible I was to him.

"Will you marry me, Ms. Jream Salicia Colton?" He fumbled with the mike as he slid a sparkling diamond on my finger. It didn't matter that I had on a silk gown I'd paid nearly $1,000 for. With tears in my eyes, I lowered myself to the floor to meet him, eye to eye. "Please be my sweet Jream."

"Jaxon," I whispered. I took the mike from his hand and switched it off. "Jaxon, I'm so sorry. . . ." The glow in his eyes suddenly went dim. In defeat he let his forehead gently press against mine, and let his lids flutter closed. "Jaxon, please look at me." It took two seconds for him to lift his lashes and meet me, pupil to pupil." A slow grin spread across my face. "I'm so sorry that you're going to ask me to marry you only once, because I want to tell you yes, not just today, but every single day for the rest of my life." Instantly the brightness reappeared in his eyes and he began to chuckle. "Yes," I confirmed. "Yes, I'll marry you." This time Jaxon threw his head back in full laughter, then brought his lips to meet mine, wrapping his arms around me as if he never wanted to let me go.

"I love you, Jream."

"I love you too, Jaxon." The crowd around us applauded as Tweet and Michetta rushed over and helped me to my feet.

Jaxon held me in his arms while Eric Benet serenaded us with "The Last Time."

"You know you hurt my feelings down there, right?"

"Yeah." I smiled. "But you know a little hurt ain't never hurt nobody."